No one, but no one manipulated him—not this avaricious bimbo, not his *perdittione* father! *No one!*

"Seems to me you don't have a choice, Rafaello, *cara*," she said bitingly. "You need a wife in a hurry—well, that's fine by me—but I won't be hemmed in by a stupid prenuptial!"

"Your choice."

"And just *what* do you think you're going to do for a precious bride, huh?" The voice behind him was taunting and vicious. He didn't even bother to turn around.

"I'm going to marry the first woman I see," he answered silkily, and was gone.

Julia James

THE ITALIAN'S TOKEN WIFE

ITALIAN
HUSBANDS

HARLEQUIN®

TORONTO • NEW YORK • LONDON
AMSTERDAM • PARIS • SYDNEY • HAMBURG
STOCKHOLM • ATHENS • TOKYO • MILAN • MADRID
PRAGUE • WARSAW • BUDAPEST • AUCKLAND

ISBN 0-373-12440-6

THE ITALIAN'S TOKEN WIFE

First North American Publication 2005.

Copyright © 2003 by Julia James.

www.eHarlequin.com

Printed in U.S.A.

CHAPTER ONE

'WHAT the hell do you mean, you won't sign?'

Rafaello di Viscenti glared down at the woman in his bed. She was a voluptuous blonde with flowing locks and celestial blue eyes, her naked body scantily covered by the duvet.

Amanda Bonham slid one slim, exposed thigh over the other, and widened her eyes.

'It's so *sordid*, darling—signing a pre-nup,' she said purringly.

Rafaello's sculpted mouth tightened.

'You agreed to all the terms in the pre-nup. Your lawyer went through it with me. Why are you balking at it now?'

Amanda pouted up at him. 'Raf, darling, we don't need a pre-nup! Wasn't last night good for you?' Her voice had gone husky, and she let a little smile play around her generous mouth. 'I can make it that good—every night.'

She nestled back into the pillows invitingly and slid her legs again, simultaneously letting the duvet slip to reveal one delectable breast.

'I can make it that good right now,' she went on, her eyes lingering over her lover's lean, honed body, with her sensual gaze openly stripping him of his extremely expensive hand-made suit of such superbly elegant tailoring that it screamed a top designer name.

Rafaello slashed an impatient hand through the air. He was immune to Amanda's plentiful bedroom charms—he'd had his fill of them for most of the night, and enough was enough.

'I don't have time for this, Amanda. Just sign the damn

5

document, as you said you would—' In his obvious anger his Italian accent was pronounced.

The inviting look vanished from the blue eyes, which were suddenly as hard as jewels.

'No,' said Amanda, yanking the duvet over her breast with a sharp motion. 'You want to marry me—you do it without a ridiculous pre-nuptial contract.'

Her lush mouth set in an obstinate line.

Rafaello swore beneath his breath, drawing on his extensive range of native Italian vocabulary unfit for polite society. He really, really could do without this.

His obsidian eyes bored into his bride-to-be.

'Amanda, *cara*,' he said with heavy patience, 'I have explained this to you already. I want a temporary bride only—you've gone into this with your eyes open; I have never attempted to deceive you. I want a bride for six months and then a swift, painless divorce. In exchange you get living expenses—very generous ones—for half a year, following one brief…very brief…visit to Italy, and you leave the marriage with a lavish pay-off. A pre-agreed lavish pay-off. *Capisce?*'

'Oh, I *capisce* all right!' Amanda's voice sounded hard. 'And now you can *capisce* me! The only pre-nup I'll sign is one with twice the pay-off!'

Rafaello stilled. So that was the way it was. She was upping the ante. He should have seen it coming. Amanda Bonham might be the ultimate airhead, but she had a homing instinct for money.

But no one, *no one* manipulated him—not this avaricious bimbo, not his *perdittione* father. *No one.*

A shutter came down over his face, and his olive-toned features became expressionless.

'Too bad.' His voice was implacable. Anyone who had ever done business with him would have known at that point to back off and give in if they still wanted to do a deal with Rafaello di Viscenti. Amanda was not so wise. Her blue eyes flashed.

'Seems to me you don't have a choice, Rafaello, *cara*,' she said bitingly. 'You need a wife in a hurry—well, that's fine by me—but I won't be hemmed in by a stupid pre-nup!'

He answered with a careless shrug as he made to turn away. 'Your choice.' He glanced back at her. 'I'll phone for a taxi for you.'

He walked across to the pier table set against the wall of the bedroom and picked up his mobile. Amanda scrambled out of bed.

'Now, wait just a minute—' she began.

Unperturbed, Rafaello went on punching numbers into the phone.

'Deal's off, *cara*. Better get your clothes on.'

A hand clawed over the fine suiting of his sleeve.

'You can't do this. You need me.'

He brushed her off as though she were a pesky fly.

'Wrong.' There was adamantine beneath the accent. 'Joe?' His voice changed. 'Call a cab, will you? About ten minutes.'

He glanced back to where the naked blonde stood quivering in outrage in his bedroom. Casually he slipped the phone inside his breast pocket.

'You can cool down under a shower—but make it quick.'

He turned to head to the double doors that led out into the rest of the apartment.

'And just *what* do you think you're going to do for a precious bride, huh?'

The voice behind him was taunting, and vicious. He didn't even bother to turn round.

'I'm going to marry the first woman I see,' he answered silkily, and was gone.

Magda flexed her tired fingers in the rubber gloves and set to work in the lavish marble-walled bathroom, wishing she didn't feel like death warmed up. Benji had been awake for two hours in the night—his sleep patterns were hopeless—but at least, she thought, smothering a yawn and brushing back a rogue wisp of hair from her forehead with the back of her wrist as she paused in rubbing at the porcelain with her cleaning sponge, it meant he was sleeping now.

A frown furrowed her brow. She wasn't going to be able to keep going with this job for much longer, she knew. While Benji had been younger it had been simple enough to carry him round with her, propping him up in his folding lightweight baby chair while she cleaned other people's luxury apartments, but now he was toddling he hated being strapped in and confined. He wanted to be out exploring—but in apartments like this, where everything from the carpets to the saucepans was excruciatingly expensive, that was just impossible.

She squirted cleaning fluid under the rim and sighed again. What kind of job could you do with a toddler in tow? Leaving him with a minder while she worked was pointless—what she earned would go to pay for the childcare. If she had any kind of decent accommodation she could be a childminder herself, and make some money by looking after other people's children as well as her own little boy, but what mother would want to park her child in the dump she lived in? Even she hated Benji being in the drab, dingy bedsit, and took him out and about as much as she could. She'd grown adept at making the hours pass in places like libraries, parks and supermarkets—anywhere that was free.

A smile softened her tired face. Benji—the light of her life, the joy of her heart. Her dearest, dearest son…

He was worth everything, *everything* to her, and there was nothing she would not do, she vowed, for his sake.

Rafaello strode angrily across the wide landing towards the open-tread staircase that led down to the reception level of the duplex apartment. Damn Amanda for trying to hold him to ransom. And damn his father for putting him in this impossible position in the first place.

His jaw tightened. Why couldn't his father accept there was no way he was going to be forced to marry his cousin Lucia and provide the rich husband she craved? Oh, she had looks, all right, but she was vain and avaricious and her temper was vicious—though she veiled it successfully enough from his father, who was now convinced she would make the perfect bride for his recalcitrant son. When orders and lamentations hadn't worked, his father had stooped to the final threat—selling Viscenti AG from under his son's nose. *Dio*, Lucia knew every weak spot a man had—from his father's obsession with getting the next-generation Viscenti heir to his own determination to keep Viscenti AG in the family. She'd played on both like a maestro.

His father's parting words rang in Rafaello's ears. 'I want you married or I sell up. And don't think I won't. But—' the older man's voice had turned cunning '—present your bride to me before your thirtieth birthday and I make the company over to you the same day.'

Well, thought Rafaello grimly, he would, indeed, present his bride to his father on his thirtieth birthday. But not the bride his parent had in mind…

A bride that would meet the letter of his father's ultimatum, but nothing more.

Anger spurted through him again. Amanda Bonham would have been the perfect bride to parade in front of his father—a fitting punishment for forcing his son to this pass. She'd have sent the old man's blood pressure sky-high. A born bimbo, with hair longer than her skirts and nothing between her ears except conceit in her own appearance and a total devotion to spending her innumerable lovers' money.

And now she'd blown it and he was back to square one.

Looking for a bride who would infuriate his father and wipe
the smirk off Lucia's face. A frown crossed his brow. It
had been all very well calling Amanda's bluff just now,
but getting hold of a bride in a handful of weeks was going
to be a challenge—even for him.

He walked down the stairs with a lithe, rapid step, a
closed, brooding look on his face—and stopped dead.

There was a baby asleep in the middle of the hallway.

Magda gave a final wipe to the pedestal, and reached into
her cleaning box for the bottle of toilet freshener. At least
bathrooms in luxury apartments were a joy to clean. All
the fittings were new and gleaming—and top quality, of
course. On the other hand, in luxury apartments there were
always an awful lot of bathrooms—one per bedroom plus
a guest WC like this one, tucked discreetly off the huge
entrance hall.

For a moment she wondered what it must be like to live
in an apartment like this. To be so rich you could have a
two-storeyed flat as big as a house, overlooking the River
Thames, with a terrace as big as a garden. The rich, Magda
thought wryly, really were different.

Not that she ever saw the inhabitants. Cleaners were only
allowed into the apartments when the owners were absent.

She flicked open the cap of the toilet freshener bottle and
upended it, ready to squirt the contents generously into the
bowl.

'What are you doing here?'

The deep, displeased voice behind her came out of the
blue, and made her jump out of her skin. The reflex action
made her squeeze the bottle prematurely, and turquoise
fluid spurted out of the bottle onto the marble floor.

With a cry of dismay Magda fell on the blue puddle and
mopped it furiously with her cleaning sponge.

'I spoke to you—answer me!'

The voice behind her sounded even more displeased. Hurriedly Magda swivelled round, and stared up.

A man stood in the doorway of the bathroom, looking down at her. Magda stared back, blinking blindly. Her dismay deepened into horror. The apartment was supposed to be empty. The caretaker had told her so. Yet here, obviously, was someone who definitely did *not* use service lifts.

And he was quite plainly furious. With dismay etched on every feature, she just went on kneeling beside the toilet pedestal, cleaning sponge in her hand.

'I'm very sorry, sir,' she managed to croak, knowing she had to sound servile for someone like this, even though it was not her fault that she was where she apparently should not have been. 'I was told it was all right to clean in here this morning.'

The man's mouth tightened.

'There is a baby in the hall,' he informed her.

With one part of her brain Magda registered that the man could not be English. Not only was his skin tone too olive-hued, but his voice was definitely accented. Spanish? Italian? Too pale to be Middle-Eastern, he must definitely be Mediterranean, she decided.

'Well?' The interrogative demand came again.

Clumsily Magda scrambled to her feet. She could not go on kneeling on the floor indefinitely.

'He's mine,' she blurted.

Something that might have been a flash of irritation showed in the man's dark eyes.

'So I had assumed. What is it doing there? This is no place for a baby!'

A child that age should be at home, not being dragged around at this hour of the day? What kind of mother was this girl? Irresponsible, obviously!

'I'm very sorry,' she said again, swallowing, hoping some more abject servility would soften his annoyance at finding her cleaning when he was in residence. Clearly he was furious his pristine apartment was being cluttered up by something as messy as a baby. She bent to pick up her cleaning box, cast a swift glance around the bathroom to make sure it was decent, and said, as meekly as she could manage, 'I'll go now, sir. I'm very sorry for having disturbed you.'

She made for the door and he stood aside to let her pass. It was uncomfortable passing him so close. He was so immaculately attired, obviously freshly washed and showered, and she had just spent several hours cleaning. She was dirty and sweaty, and she had a horrible feeling she smelt as bad as she felt. She hurried out to Benji, who, blessedly, was still asleep, and made to scoop up his chair.

'Wait!'

The order was imperative, and Magda halted instinctively, Benji a heavy weight on her arm. Hesitantly she turned round.

The man was looking at her. Staring at her.

Magda froze, as if she were a rabbit caught in headlights. Or rather an antelope realising a leopard had just come out of the undergrowth.

Oh, help, she thought silently. Now what?

Rafaello let his gaze rest on the girl. She was slightly built, drab in the extreme, with hair the colour of mud and unmemorable features. She also—his nose wrinkled in disdain—smelt of sweat and cleaning fluids. There was a smut of dirt on her cheek. She looked about twenty or so.

He found himself glancing at her hands. They were covered by yellow rubber gloves. He frowned. His gaze went back to her face. She was looking at him with a look of deepest apprehension.

'You don't have to bolt like a frightened rabbit,' he said. Deliberately he made his voice less brusque, though it didn't seem to alter her expression a jot. She still stood there, poised for flight, baby in one hand, cleaning materials in the other.

Rafaello took a couple of steps towards her.

'Tell me—are you married?'

The brusqueness was back in his voice. He didn't mean it to be, but it was. It was because part of his mind was telling him that he was completely mad, thinking what he was thinking. But he was thinking it all the same...

A blank look came into the girl's eyes, as if he had asked her an unintelligible question.

'Well?' demanded Rafaello. The woman seemed beyond answering him.

Jerkily, the woman shook her head, her eyes still with that fixed, blank look to them. Rafaello's gaze focussed on her more intently. So, she wasn't married—he hadn't thought so, even without being able to see if she wore a wedding ring. And despite the baby.

His eyes glanced across to the sleeping infant. He wasn't any good at telling the ages of babies, but this one looked quite big. Too big for that chair, in fact. It was dark-haired, head lolling forward, totally out for the count.

But a baby was good—however irresponsible the mother! A baby was very good, he mused consideringly. So was the rest of her. Once again his eyes flickered over her, taking in the full drabness of her appearance, and he thought he could see her wince.

'Boyfriend?'

Her eyes widened and then went even blanker. With the same jerky movement she shook her head. She also, Rafaello spotted, edged very slightly closer to the front door. He frowned. Why was she being so jumpy?

'I have a business proposition to put to you.' His voice was clipped as he banked down the anger at his predicament that still roiled within him like an injured tiger.

A noise came from her that might have been a whimper, but that seemed unlikely since there was no reason for such a sound. Rafaello walked to the door leading into the kitchen and held it open with the flat of his hand.

'In here.' He gestured.

The strangled croaking noise came again, and this time the woman definitely shrank back towards the door.

'I have to go!' Her voice came out high and squawky. 'I'm very sorry!'

Rafaello frowned again. Just then a door slammed on the upper floor. The next moment Amanda was descending as fast as her four-inch heels and very tight short skirt would permit. As she saw the tableau below her face lit up with a vicious smile.

'Why, Raf, darling,' she purred venomously, 'how galling for you. ''The first woman I see''.' She gave a bad imitation of his Italian accent. 'And that's what you get. Bad luck.'

The man's accented voice answered the woman. He was purring, too, but it was the purr of a big cat, and it made the hairs stand up on the nape of Magda's neck.

'Yes, indeed, Amanda, *cara*, and she is just perfect for me.'

The look that crossed the other woman's face was a picture. Fury mingled with disbelief.

'You're joking. You have to be.'

For his answer, Rafaello simply lifted one darkly arched eyebrow and gave the woman a mocking look.

'Your taxi will be waiting downstairs, *cara*. Time to go.'

For a moment the woman just stood there, fizzing with fury. Then with a tightening of her face she marched to the front door, shoved Magda aside, and flung it open.

'Wait!' squawked Magda, and tried to rush after her. What possible reason could the apartment owner have for wanting to know if she were married or had a boyfriend? No good ones she could think of—and plenty that were bad. She'd heard enough stories from other cleaners about men who liked forcing their attentions on vulnerable women in lowly jobs.

'Get away from me, you disgusting creature,' snapped the other woman. She stormed off. Desperately Magda tried to catch the front door, but it was taken from her abruptly.

'I said I had a business proposition for you. Have the courtesy to hear me out.' The accented voice dropped into a sardonic range. 'It could be to your financial advantage.'

Magda flung him a terrified look. Oh, God, she was right. He was about to make some kind of obscene proposition. 'No, thank you—I don't do that sort of thing.'

The man frowned again. 'You do not know what I am about to ask you,' he countered brusquely.

'Whatever it is, I don't do it. I'm just a cleaner. It's all I do.' Her voice was a squawk again. 'Please, let me go— please. I do the cleaning. That's all.'

The man's expression changed suddenly, as if he finally realised the reason for her near panic.

'You misunderstand me.' His voice was arctic. 'The business proposition I want you to consider has nothing to do with sex.'

Magda stared at him, taking in his expensive male gorgeousness. Reality came back with a vengeance. Of course a man like him would not sexually proposition a woman like her. Seeing herself through those disdainful eyes, suddenly she felt as if she were two inches high. Mortification flooded through her.

Abruptly, she felt the weight of her cleaning box taken from her.

'Come into the kitchen,' said the man, 'and I will explain.'

Magda sat, completely frozen, on one of the high stools set against the kitchen bar. Benji miraculously slept on, snug in his baby chair on the floor.

'Say…say that again?' she asked faintly.

'I will pay you the sum of one hundred thousand pounds,' the man spelt out in clipped, accented tones, 'for you to be married to me—quite legally—for six months, at the end of which period we shall file for divorce by mutual consent. You will need to accompany me to Italy for…legal reasons. Then you will return here, and your living expenses will be paid by me. On our divorce you will receive one hundred thousand pounds, no more. Do you understand?'

No, thought Magda. I don't understand. All I understand is that you're nuts.

But it seemed unwise to point this out to the man sitting on the other side of the bar from her. She was acutely, utterly uncomfortable being here. And not just because the man was making such an absurd proposition to her.

It was also because he was, quite simply, the most devastating male she had ever seen—inside or outside the covers of a glossy magazine. He had lean, slim looks, very Italian, but with an edge about him that kept his heart-stoppingly handsome face from looking soft. He had beauty, all right, but it was male beauty, honed and planed, and the long eyelashes swept past obsidian eyes that had an incredibly dangerous appeal to them.

'You don't believe me, do you?'

The question caught her on the hop, interrupting her rapt, if surreptitious gazing at him, and all she could do was open her mouth and then close it again.

A tight, humourless smile twisted at his mouth, changing the angles of his face. Something detonated deep inside Magda, but she had no time to pay any attention to it. He was speaking again.

'I would be the first to concede the situation is…bizarre. But, nevertheless—' he spread his hands above the bar, and Magda noticed how beautiful they were, long and slender, with a steely strength to them despite their immaculate manicure '—I do, as it happens, require a wife at very short notice, for a very particular purpose. Perhaps I should point out,' he went on, in a voice that made her feel ashamed of her own lack of physical appeal in the presence of a man with such a super-abundance of it, 'that the marriage will be in name only. Tell me, do you have a passport?'

Magda shook her head. A look of irritation crossed the man's face, then he moved his right hand dismissively. 'No matter. These things can be arranged in time. Now, what about your child's father? Is he still on the scene?'

Magda tried to think what on earth to say, but failed miserably.

'I thought not.' The expression of unconcealed disdain for her child's fatherless state silenced her even more than her inability to provide an answer under such circumstances. 'But that is all to the good,' he swept on. 'He will not interfere.'

A dark glance swept over her, as if he were making some kind of final internal decision. 'So, altogether, I can see no obstacles to what I propose—you are clearly extremely suitable.'

Panic struck Magda. He was sweeping ahead, dragging her along as if she were nothing more than a tin can rattling on a piece of string behind a racing car. She had to stop all this right now. It was too absurd for words.

'Please,' she cut in, 'I'm not suitable at all, really. And I'm sorry, but I have to go now. I have other apartments to clean and I'm running late—'

She didn't, this was the last one, but there was no need to let him know that.

His voice came silkily.

'If you accept my proposition you will never clean another apartment in your life. For a woman of your background you will live in comfortable circumstances—if you are financially prudent—for several years simply on what I shall pay you for six months of your life.'

Emotions warred inside Magda. Uppermost was umbrage

at the way he had said so disdainfully 'a woman of your background', as though she came from a different species of humanity. But beneath that, forcing its way to the surface, was something more powerful.

Temptation.

Comfortable circumstances...

The phrase jumped out at her. What on earth had the man said—something about a hundred thousand pounds? It couldn't be true. The thought of so much money was beyond her. With a hundred thousand pounds she could move out of London, buy a flat, even a little house, stop having to depend on state income support, stop work, look after Benji properly...plan for the future.

For a moment, so intense that it hurt, she had a vision of herself and Benji in a nice little house somewhere, with a little garden, on a nice road, and nice families all around. Nothing spectacular, just normal and ordinary and...nice. Somewhere decent to bring him up. Somewhere that was a real home.

She saw herself in the kitchen, baking cakes, while she watched Benji tricycle round a little paved patio, with a swing-set on the lawn beyond, a cat snoozing on the windowsill, washing hanging on the line. With next-door neighbours who had children, and hung up their washing, and baked cakes. Who lived normal, ordinary lives.

An ache of longing so deep inside it made her feel weak swept through her.

Across the bar, Rafaello's dark eyes narrowed. She was taking the bait; he could see. It had been hard work to get her to this point—far harder than he had envisaged. But at last she was responding.

And the more time and effort he put into persuading her, the more he was convinced she was perfect for the job.

Dio, but his father would be apoplectic! His son presenting him with a bride who had a fatherless kid in tow and who cleaned toilets for a living. Who looked as drab

and plain as the back end of a bus. That would teach him
to try and force his hand—

Magda saw the gleam of triumph in the obsidian eyes
and quailed. She must be insane even to *think* of thinking
about what he had offered her! A hundred thousand
pounds—it was ridiculous. It was absurd. Almost as absurd
as the notion of a female like her marrying a man like
that…for whatever lunatic reason.

'I really do have to go,' she said with a rush, and got to
her feet. As she did so she must have jogged Benji's chair,
because he gave a sudden start and woke up. Immediately
he gave out a little wail. Magda stooped down and cupped
his cheek. 'It's OK, Benji. Mum's here.'

The wail stopped, and Benji reached out one of his little
hands and patted her face. Then, promptly, he started wrig-
gling mightily, trying to free himself from his bonds.

'It's all right, muffin, we're just going.' She hefted him
up onto her arm, shifting her leg to balance the weight. She
picked up her cleaning box with her other hand.

'I'll…er…let myself out…' she said awkwardly to the
man who had just asked her to marry him, and who was
still sitting on the other side of the bar, watching her
through assessing eyes.

'A hundred thousand pounds. No more cleaning. No
more having to take your son around like this. It's no life
for him.'

His words fell like stones into her conscience—pricking
it and destroying it at the same time.

'This isn't real,' she said suddenly, her voice sounding
harsh. 'It can't be. It's just nuts, the whole thing!'

The thin, humourless smile twisted his mouth again. 'If
it's any comfort, I feel the same way. But—' he took a
deep, sharply inhaled breath '—if I don't turn up next
month with a wife, everything I have worked for will be
wasted. And I will not permit that.'

There was a chill in his words as he finished that made her shiver. But what could she say?

Nothing. She could only go. At her side, Benji wriggled and started to whimper.

'I'm sorry,' she said helplessly, but whether to Benji or this unbelievable man with his unbelievable proposition, she didn't know.

Then she got out of the apartment like a bat out of hell.

Music thumped through the thin walls of the bedsit, pounding through Magda's head. She'd had a headache all day, ever since finally making her escape from that madman's apartment.

But what he had said to her was driving her mad as well. She kept hearing it in her head—a hundred thousand pounds, a hundred thousand pounds. It drummed like the bass shuddering through from next door, tolled like a bell condemning her to a life of dreary, grinding, no-hope poverty.

Would she ever get a decent home of her own? The council waiting list was endless, and in the meantime she was stuck here, in this bleak, grimy bedsit. When Benji had been a baby it hadn't been so bad. But now that he was getting older his horizons were broadening—he needed more space; he needed a proper home. This wasn't a home—it never could be—it was barely a roof over their heads.

Not that she was ungrateful. Dear God, single mothers in other parts of the world could die in a gutter with their children without anyone caring. At least here, the state system, however imperfect, provided an umbrella for her. Not that she hadn't been pressed to give Benji up for adoption.

'Life as a single mother is very hard, Miss Jones,' the social worker had said to her. 'Even with state support. You will have a much better chance to make something of yourself without such an encumbrance.'

Encumbrance. That was the word that had done it. Made her stand up, newborn baby in her arms, and say tightly, 'Benji stays with me!'

Encumbrances. She knew all about them.

She'd been one herself. An encumbrance so great that the woman who had given birth to her had left her to die in an alley.

Well, no one, *no one*—neither man nor God—was going to take Benji from her!

Through the wall the music pounded, far too loud. None of the residents dared complain. The man with the ghetto-blaster was on drugs, everyone knew that, and could turn ugly at the drop of a pin. Eventually he would turn it off, but often not till the early hours. No wonder Benji had broken sleep patterns.

Knowing there was no way she could get him to sleep, even though it was gone eight in the evening, Magda let him play. He was sitting beside her on the lumpy bed, quite happily posting shapes through the holes in a plastic tower and gurgling with pleasure every time he got it right. It was a good toy, and Magda had been pleased to find it in a charity shop. All Benji's toys and clothes—and her own clothes and possessions—came from charity shops and jumble sales.

As she played with him, trying to ignore the pounding music, her mind went round and round, thinking about that extraordinary encounter this morning.

Had it actually happened? Had a man who looked like every woman's fantasy Latin millionaire really suggested she marry him for six months and thereby earn a hundred thousand pounds? It was so insane surely it couldn't have happened.

The knock on her door made her start. On the bed, Benji looked round interrogatively. The knock came again.

'Miss Jones?'

The voice was muffled and she could hardly hear it

through the racket coming from next door. Was it the land-lord? He turned up from time to time to check up on his property, from which he made a substantial living by letting it out to those on state benefits. Cautiously she went to the door. She'd fitted a chain herself, not feeling in the slightest secure with neighbours like hers.

Bracing her weight against the back of the door, ready to slam it shut, she opened it a crack.

'Yes?'

'It's Rafaello di Viscenti. We spoke this morning. Please be so good as to admit me.'

CHAPTER TWO

TOTAL astonishment made her obey. As she opened the door to him Rafaello experienced a momentary qualm. Could he really go through with this? Marry this…this… what was the English word for it…? Skivvy? Even for the reasons he had. Seeing her again brought home just how dire she was. She was wearing a saggy sweatshirt and baggy trousers, her stringy, mud-coloured hair was scraped back, and her face was gaunt, with hollows under her eyes. She was, he could safely say, the most physically repellent female he'd ever set eyes on.

But that is what makes her so perfect. OK, so she was the antithesis of Amanda, his first choice, but now, instead of a sexy, airhead bimbo he could take home this plain-as-sin, single mother! It would work just as well—if not better.

Besides—the thought came to him with a stab of discomfort as his quick glance took in the dump she lived in and finally settled on the baby sitting on the bed, staring at him with big, chocolate eyes—she could certainly do with the money more than Amanda could…

'What…what are you doing here? How…how did you find me?'

The girl was stammering, clearly in a state of shock. Rafaello stepped inside and shut the door behind him. She shrank back, getting between him and the baby.

Rafaello frowned. *Dio*, did she think he was going to harm her child?

'There is no need to panic,' he said in a dry voice. 'I found you, Miss Jones, through the cleaning agency you work for, that is all. And I have been waiting to speak to

23

you again all day. You have only just been reported back here. Where have you been?'

He made it sound as if she'd been absent without leave.

'Out,' said Magda faintly, backing away to the bed so she could snatch up Benji in a moment if she had to. 'I don't spend much time here.'

Her visitor made a derisive noise in his throat. 'That I can understand. Where is that music coming from?' he demanded, glaring around.

'The room next door. He likes it loud.'

'It is intolerable!' announced Rafaello.

Yes, agreed Magda, but all the same I have to tolerate it, and so does everyone else in the house. She was still in a state of shock, she knew. She had almost persuaded herself that the unbelievable events of the morning had never happened. Now, like something out of a dream, the man was standing in front of her again.

Rafaello di Viscenti... The name rolled around her brain like a verbal caress. The name suited him absolutely, she realised, perfectly complementing the image he presented of the luxury-class Italian male.

She blinked, realising she was staring at him gormlessly. He crossed to the table in the room, which served as dining table and general work surface, and placed an elegant leather document case down upon it, from which he proceeded to withdraw a wad of documents.

'I have had the requisite papers drawn up,' he informed her. 'Please read them before you sign them.'

Magda swallowed. 'Er...I'm not signing anything, Mr Viscenti.'

'Di Viscenti,' he said. 'You will be Signora di Viscenti. You must learn the correct form of address.'

Magda rubbed the suddenly damp palms of her hands surreptitiously on her trousers. 'Um...Mr di Viscenti, I...er...I...er...don't think I can help you. Really. It's all a bit too...er...*weird* for me...'

She cast around in her mind desperately, trying to find a tactful way of saying that the whole thing was so flaky she wouldn't touch it with a bargepole.

His arched eyebrows rose. 'Weird?' he echoed. Then, brusquely, he nodded. 'Yes, it is weird, Miss Jones. But, as I explained to you this morning, I have no choice—it is a matter of who controls our family business, Viscenti AG, the details of which need not trouble you. But it is sufficient reason for me to require a very temporary marriage, under very controlled circumstances, to meet certain…conditions…that amount to nothing more than an empty legality. It is a mere formal exercise for which, unfortunately, my marriage—even though a temporary one—is necessary.'

'But why to me?' she burst out. 'A man like you could pick any woman to marry.'

Rafaello accepted the ingenuous compliment as nothing more than the obvious. 'Think of my proposition not as a marriage, but as a job, Miss Jones. A very temporary job.' His voice became dry. 'That was something the previous…candidate…found difficult to accept.' He made a very Italian gesture with his hand. 'The woman you encountered this morning?' he prompted.

'You were going to marry *her*?'

'Yes. Unfortunately she…withdrew at the last moment. Hence,' he went on with heavy civility, 'my urgent need for a replacement. I must marry as soon as possible.'

'But why *me*?' Magda persisted. It still seemed so totally absurd. However, she had to admit that the knowledge that he had been on the point of entering into this weird marriage he wanted with that underdressed cow who had stormed out of his apartment this morning did make what he was proposing more credible. But it still left his choice of herself as a replacement incredible. After all, surely a man like that would know women like that first one by the score.

'Because there is one essential difference between you…and women like her. Amanda *wanted* the money I was going to pay her. You…' He paused and looked at her, and his eyes suddenly seemed to see right into the heart of her. 'You *need* the money. That makes you more… reliable.'

Magda stilled.

Remorselessly he went on.

'You do need the money, Miss Jones. You need it desperately. You need it to save you—and your child.' His dark eyes held hers, holding her as if he were the devil himself. Tempting her beyond endurance. 'You can't go on living here—you know you can't. You have to get out— you know that. My money will let you do that. It's a life-raft for you—and your child. Take it—take the money I'm offering you.'

Her face had paled. He could see the emotions working. Ruthlessly, as if he were driving yet another hard-nosed business deal, he pressed his advantage. The thump of the music vibrated in every stick of furniture in the shabby bedsit.

'I hold the key to a new life for you—a new future—in exchange for four weeks of your life now. That's all I ask of you in exchange. A month in my company—and then you are free. Free—with enough money to get you out of here for ever…'

His eyes were boring into hers. She couldn't think, couldn't feel. Could hardly breathe.

'I…I don't know who you are… You could be anyone…' Her voice was faint.

His chin tilted with an inborn arrogance that had been bred into his genes. She could see that.

'I am Rafaello di Viscenti. The di Viscentis are a family of the utmost respectability and antiquity. I am chief executive of Viscenti AG. It is a company valued at well over four hundred million euros. I do not usually—' there was a distinct bite in his voice '—have to present my credentials.'

Magda swallowed. 'Yes, well,' she mumbled, 'I don't exactly move in those circles...'

'And the offer I have made you,' he went on, with that same edge of hauteur in his voice, 'is exactly what I have outlined to you. There are no hidden clauses, no tricks to deceive you. You may talk everything through with my lawyers if you wish. What is in those papers—' he gestured with his hand to the documents on the table '—is what you will get. Now, tell me, if you please, what is stopping you from signing them?'

You, she wanted to shout. It's *you*. She stared at him wildly. I can't marry a man who looks like you, who's as rich as you, who's as gorgeous as you—I can't marry a man, no matter what for, or how temporarily, who looks as if he's stepped out of a celebrity mag. It's absurd. It's nuts. It's...

A wail distracted her. Benji, bored with posting shapes, had knocked over the tower and started to howl. Automatically Magda collapsed back on the bed and lifted him up to her knees, hugging his firm little body. The sobs ceased, and Benji twisted round in her lap to pay some attention to the stranger in the middle of the room. Magda's arms wrapped round him, and she felt his little heart beat against hers.

'A hundred thousand pounds,' said Rafaello softly. 'Think...*think*...what you could do with it...'

Magda's body started to rock... Go away, she thought desperately, *go away*. Take your designer suit and your expensive briefcase and go...go before I give in, before you tempt me like Lucifer himself...

'You wouldn't be doing it for yourself. You'd be doing it for your baby.'

She shut her eyes, trying to block out that soft, seductive voice.

'If I walk out now—never to come back—how will you live with yourself? Knowing you turned down the chance to get your baby out of here, for ever?'

She went on rocking, her arms wrapped so closely around Benji that he began to protest.

'Four weeks—no more than that—in my family home in Italy, which is very respectable, Miss Jones, I do assure you—and then you're free.'

'Benji comes with me.' Her voice was high-pitched.

Rafaello spread his hands. 'Of course the baby comes with you—that is essential.' It wasn't necessary to spell out to her just why his bride should arrive accoutred with a fatherless child. 'You just have to sign the papers, that's all you have to do...' He slid his hand inside his breast pocket, taking out a gold fountain pen, slipping off the top, proffering it to her. 'Come—'

There was an imperiousness in his voice she could not resist. Slowly, as if she was sleepwalking, she slid Benji from her lap back on to the bed, ignoring his wail of protest. Slowly, very slowly, she got to her feet. It wasn't real. None of this was real. She'd wake up in a moment and find it had all been a dream.

He held the pen out to her. Numbly she took it. Numbly she looked down at the table, to where he was turning the documents to the last page and placing one long, lean finger where she should sign.

The ink flowed from the gold pen in smooth, lustrous curves, despite the halting jerkiness of her signature. In the evening light it seemed blood-coloured. As she handed it back to him, standing at her side like a dark, infernal presence, she felt a wave of weakness go through her.

What have I done? Oh, dear God, what have I done?

But whatever it was, it was too late to go back.

Magda sat, staring out of the porthole, at the sunlit cloudscape beyond. Benji was on her lap, asleep. He'd had a bad takeoff, even with sucking on the bottle of juice to ease the pressure on his little eardrums, but now, after half an hour of grizzling, he'd finally fallen asleep.

She glanced covertly across the aisle to where Rafaello di Visenti was sitting. He was working through a pile of papers laid out on the table in front of him, and so far as he was concerned, she could tell, he might as well have been alone on the plane.

There were no passengers apart from themselves on the luxurious executive jet winging its way across Europe. For Magda, who had never flown in her life, it was an experience she could hardly believe was happening.

But then her whole life since she had signed her name at Rafaello di Visenti's arrogant bidding had been completely unbelievable. She knew that if she had thought too much about what she was doing she could not have gone through with it. So she'd just let herself be swept along, let herself be that tin can racing along behind Rafaello di Visenti's powerful, unstoppable car taking her into an undreamed-of future.

Not that she'd seen him between that evening and today. Ironically, it had been his total indifference to her once he had got her to agree to marry him that had reassured her most. It was indeed, in his eyes, just a job, and she was nothing more than a junior employee. He had despatched one of his other junior employees to ensure the correct documents for their marriage were in place, to accompany her to register the marriage, and to arrange passports for her and Benji.

This morning she had been collected from her bedsit and driven to her local register office. The ceremony uniting them in matrimony had passed in a complete haze. She must have said the right things at the right time, but all she could remember now, as she sat and stared out at the sun-drenched cloudscape, was an overwhelming impression of a tall presence beside her, a deeply accented voice interspersing with hers and the registrar's, and that was that.

Only one moment stood out—when the tall presence beside her had lifted her hand and slid a gold wedding ring on her finger. Something had prickled through her like electricity. It must have been the coolness of his brief touch, nothing more. A moment later she'd been required to perform the same office for him, and to her own astonishment had realised she could hardly do so—her hand had trembled so violently.

She'd managed it somehow, all the same, and then, distracting her completely, she had heard Benji, kept back in the outer room with some more of Rafaello di Viscenti's minions, give out a mournful wail. From that moment on her sole thought had been to get back to him, and the rest of the ceremony had been lost to her.

As soon as she could she had hurried out, back to Benji, and scooped him into her arms. Then Rafaello had been beside her, taking her elbow and saying smoothly, but completely impersonally, 'If you are ready, we must go.'

A limo had whisked them to Heathrow and, apart from asking her in that same impersonal manner if she were comfortable and had everything she required, that was all her new husband had said to her. He'd seemed, Magda vaguely registered, to be quite abstracted during the whole procedure—as abstracted as she was.

The haze around her brain deepened. *Go with the flow,* she told herself, and smoothed Benji's silky hair, gazing again out of the porthole. Shock was keeping her going, she knew. Yet beneath the numbness she could feel a thread of excitement stirring. However bizarre the circumstances, she was going abroad for the first time in her life.

Italy. Could she really be going there? In the time since she had given in to Rafaello di Viscenti's imperious will she had got out as many library books as she could on the country. Reading had always been her solace, ever since

she had discovered it was a way of blotting out reality—
the reality of being brought up in care—taking her away to
magical lands, with wonderful people, a world away from
the disturbed, unhappy children that surrounded her, the
cast-off jetsam of adults too dysfunctional to be responsible
parents themselves, making their unwanted children pay the
price for their own emotional shortfalls.

As she stared out over the radiant cloudscape—another
mystical land up here, so far above the earth—her memory
fled back to Kaz. Her face clouded. Although she might
feel the desolation of a child utterly abandoned by its parents, at least Magda knew she had come off lucky com-
pared with Kaz. Kaz had had the bruises, the badly mended
bones, the haunted eyes. Taken into care to be safe from
an abusive stepfather and alcoholic mother, Kaz had been
almost as withdrawn as Magda. Perhaps it was natural the
two of them had drawn together, to form, for perhaps the
first time in either of their lives, a real friendship, a real
emotional bond.

Sorrow pierced her. She gazed out over the fleecy, sunlit
surface of the clouds. Are you out there somewhere, Kaz?
she wondered.

In her arms, Benji stirred. Gently Magda bent to kiss his
fine dark hair, her heart swelling with love. She lifted her
eyes again and stared out of the window. She had done the
right thing in agreeing to this bizarre marriage; she knew
she had. However weird this was, she was doing the right
thing for the right reason.

For Benji.

For the first time since Rafaello di Viscenti had turned
her world upside down, she felt at peace with herself for
what she had done.

The peace lasted until the plane landed. Then, in the confusion of a busy Italian airport, hanging on to a wailing
Benji, whose ears had set off again during the descent into

Pisa, Magda once more felt like that tin can rattling along a motorway.

A hand pressed, not roughly, but insistently, into the small of her back.

'This way,' said Rafaello di Viscenti, the man she had married a handful of hours ago, and guided her forward. They made their way out of the airport to where a large limousine hummed at the kerb. Within moments they were inside, luggage in the boot, and the chauffeur was drawing out into the traffic.

The journey took well over an hour, and the latter part, away from the *autostrada*, was by far the most fascinating. Magda stared out of the window, drinking in the Tuscan landscape, a world away from the rainy South London streets she had left that morning. As the car purred along she pointed things out to Benji, whose baby seat was closest to the window. She leant over him, glad of the opportunity to put as much distance between herself and the man occupying the far corner of the huge car. Since he seemed to be preoccupied with his work still, tapping away at a laptop on his knees, she assumed he preferred to be left alone.

That suited her completely. Having to make stilted conversation with him would have been much worse. Right now, she just wanted to savour being in Italy.

Talking softly to Benji, she drank it all in. Road signs in Italian, driving on the wrong side of the road, houses, cars and people—all Italian. They were steadily climbing, she realised, heading up into the hills. Summer sunlight drenched the rolling landscape, etching the cypresses like ink. She stared, entranced. Stone farmhouses and picturesque stone-built towns, olive groves and vineyards, goats and sheep grazing, and, as the road grew steeper and narrower, old men with donkeys, old women covered in black from headscarf to heavy shoes.

Finally, as the roads grew narrower and the traffic more and more sparse, the limo slowed and turned in through large ironwork gates that opened at a buzz from the chauffeur. She heard Rafaello click off his laptop and close it up.

'We are here,' he announced.

She glanced briefly across at him. His face was expressionless and, it seemed to her, particularly tense. Automatically she tensed as well. It dawned on her that the flight and car journey had been nothing more than an interlude. Now, right now, in front of others, she was about to take on the role of Signora di Viscenti.

As if reading her attack of nerves, Rafaello spoke suddenly.

'Be calm,' he instructed. 'There is nothing for you to be anxious about. For you, this is simply a job. Please remember that.'

Was she imagining it, or had a grimmer note entered his tense voice? His dark gaze flicked over her again, and something in it sent a chill through her. Instinctively, Magda felt the chill was not directed at her. But there was anger deep down in there somewhere, she knew. Anger at having been required to marry at all.

Well, she thought resolutely, that was his business, not hers. She was simply doing what he was—to put it bluntly—paying her to do. She had gone through a wedding ceremony but it was nothing more than a legal formality. She was Signora di Viscenti in nothing more than name—and she would never be anything else.

For a moment so brief it hardly existed a longing struck her, so intense it pierced like pain, that somehow, if fairytales were real, this might be one—she really was sweeping along the driveway to her new home, with a husband beside her to die for...

But fairytales weren't real. They were just...fairytales.

Nothing to do with her.

The car drew up in front of a castellated villa that made Magda's eyes widen in wonder. It was ancient—and beau-

tiful. The old stone was weathered, the huge wooden door
studded, and the grounds stretched all the way to the woods
and hills beyond.

Carefully she extracted Benji, who had been lulled off
to sleep some time ago, by the rocking motion of the car,
and clambered out with him. She held him on her hip and
gazed around. The warmth of the late afternoon after the
limo's air-conditioning struck her like a blessing, warming
her through the thin material of the cotton dress she was
wearing. It was the best she possessed, though it had cost
under five pounds in a charity shop and was a size too large
for her. Its low-waisted, button-fronted style, she knew,
would probably have suited a matron of fifty better than
herself. But what did it matter? If Rafaello di Viscenti had
objected to it he would have got one of his minions to
arrange an alternative.

'Come—' The man she had married that morning slipped
a hand under her elbow. There was a tension in his grip
that communicated itself to her and to Benji, who gave a
little grizzle.

Magda suffered a swift glance at Rafaello's face. Its expression was closed and shuttered, and looked, she thought,
very remote. Instinctively she realised that she and Benji
were the last things on his mind.

As they approached the front door it swung open suddenly, and a man came out. He was elderly, dressed in
shirtsleeves and a waistcoat, and she realised he must be
some sort of butler. He greeted Rafaello, and though she
could understand not a word she could tell he had definitely
not been expecting his arrival.

And certainly not hers.

More rapid Italian followed, and Magda was sure she
was not imagining the strong disapproval in the man's reaction—nor the shocked expression when he took in not
just her, but Benji, too. Rafaello, she could tell, was simply

terse and uncommunicative—and definitely not pleased by
something the man had said to him.

Then they were indoors and Rafaello was turning to her.
'You and the child must be tired. I am sure you would
like to rest a while. Come.' His voice was impersonal.

They proceeded up a grand staircase, and Magda could
not help staring bug-eyed around her. The inside of the
house was as beautiful as the outside, with white plain plaster walls hung with tapestries and oil paintings, and a marble staircase edged with scrolling wrought-iron banisters.
Everything looked incredibly antique and expensive, a
world away from the modern luxury apartments she
cleaned.

Disbelief welled through her again—she was going to
live *here* for the next few weeks? This was definitely a
fairytale!

Rafaello took her into a large room leading off the broad
upper landing. Again she just gazed around, wide-eyed. A
vast carved wooden bed dominated the room, which was
filled with huge pieces of furniture but, such was the size
of the room, there was no sense of being cramped at all. A
fabulous Persian carpet spread out beneath her feet, and
heavy drapes cascaded to the floor either side of the pair
of shuttered windows. A huge stone fireplace faced the bed.

'The *en suite* bathroom is through that door,' Rafaello
informed her in the same terse, blank tone. 'Do you have
all that you need for yourself and the child? Giuseppe will
obtain anything you ask him for.'

She managed to nod, feeling incredibly awkward. The
butler-type—Giuseppe, she presumed—had followed them
up, and now came in, carrying her suitcase from the limo.
Its shabbiness looked as out of place here as she did.

'Good,' said Rafaello. He glanced at his watch. 'Refresh
yourself, and the child. Would you like some coffee?'

She nodded. 'Th-thank you,' she stammered faintly.

'Good,' he said again. 'Giuseppe will show you downstairs in a while, when you are rested. Oh…' He paused, and his eyes flicked over her again, unreadably. 'There is no need for you to change.'

Then he was gone, and Giuseppe with him.

Alone, Magda gazed around again. It was obvious that she was simply being stashed away until required, but she could hardly complain about her storage conditions. The room was exquisite. Her only worry was that everything in it was far too precious for her and Benji.

Benji, however, was eager to be mobile. She put him down and he promptly tottered off, eagerly exploring this new environment. She watched him head for the huge bed. She would not have to ask for a cot—the bed was easily big enough for her and Benji.

And her husband?

She pushed the thought away. Rafaello di Viscenti was her husband by nothing more than a legal sleight-of-hand. Where he slept had nothing to do with her.

Rafaello walked back down the staircase, his expression tight. He did not look forward to the imminent confrontation, but it was both inevitable and essential. He had to teach his father, once and for all, that he was not a puppet with strings to be pulled.

For his father Viscenti AG, founded over a hundred years ago to restore the ailing fortunes of a landed family, was simply a business, yielding a more than comfortable living for the di Viscentis.

Rafaello knew better. The world had shifted—globalisation was the name of the game. The only game. Viscenti AG had to move into the twenty-first century, and the only way to do that was to become major league on a global stage. The euro was seeing to that, if nothing else—Europe was wide open, and the blast of competition blew with a chillier wind than ever. Cosy family businesses just wouldn't survive.

Up till now Rafaello had had to fight for his strategy of taking Viscenti AG global every inch of the way with his father. He might be chief executive, but his father was chairman, and owned the majority shareholding. He had looked with grudging disapproval upon all Rafaello's endless labours in opening up the European market to the company, and, even though turnover and profits were soaring, Rafaello knew his father wished Viscenti AG had stayed the native enterprise it always had been.

But Rafaello had worked his backside off for the company he had so dramatically expanded, and he was not, *not* about to see his efforts wasted—or the family company sold off to strangers.

To prevent that he would do anything—whatever it took.

As he had proved that morning.

He strode across the marble-floored hallway and into the book-lined library he used as an office. Crossing to the window that overlooked the ornamental pool with its trickling fountain, Rafaello pushed back the sides of his suit jacket and splayed his fingers along his hips, looking out moodily. Typical of his father not to be here when he wanted him to be. Giuseppe had informed him, when he'd arrived, that both his father and cousin had gone out for lunch and were not expected back until late afternoon. He'd then promptly gone on to try and discover who the young female with the baby was.

Rafaello had cut him off, refusing to be drawn. The girl's identity was going to be a surprise for everyone. Oh, yes, certainly a surprise. He gave a grim smile. She was, just as he had anticipated, ideal. She'd stared around open-mouthed as he'd taken her upstairs, as though she'd landed on an alien planet, her child hitched on her hip, her cheap, wrong-sized, unflattering dress hanging on her skinny body, her complexion pasty and her mud-coloured hair scraped back.

His smile tightened. His father would be incandescent

with rage—not just at having been outmanoeuvred, but at having the name of di Viscenti so totally insulted by his own son presenting him with such a female for a daughter-in-law.

A momentary frown creased his brow, then it cleared. The girl could have no idea of what made her so ideal for his purposes—and, besides, she was being paid what was for her a vast sum of money, had entered into the arrangement of her own free will. So far she had done exactly what he wanted—which was, predominantly, to do what she was told, ask no questions and keep out of the way until required.

He turned away from the window and sat himself down at his desk. He might as well get some work done while he was waiting. It might distract him from the coming confrontation.

Why did it have to be like this? he wondered, his expression drawn. Why this unnecessary, painful showdown with his father? Why couldn't he simply talk to him—communicate instead of confront?

He sighed. He'd had more communication in the last fifteen years with Giuseppe and his wife Maria. It had been they who'd seen him through from adolescence to adulthood—Giuseppe, who'd doused his morning-after head before his father saw him; Maria, who'd refused to hand him the keys of his first sports car when he'd been too angry to drive after another explosive head-to-head with his father. And it had been Giuseppe who'd listened to him when he'd expounded his dreams of making Viscenti AG a global name, Maria who'd rung a peal over him for leaving a trail of besotted girls behind him, making him wise up and stick to society women.

He knew his father considered him dissolute—hence his determination to force him into matrimony. His mouth tightened. If there had been *any* real hope of communication with his father he would not have had to do what he

had done this morning. A shadow crossed his eyes. It was
his mother's death in a road accident when he was fifteen
that had caused the rift between father and son. They had
both grieved—but not together. His father, mourning his
adored wife, had withdrawn, cutting off his son. And
Rafaello knew, with the hindsight of his thirty years, that
the wild behaviour he had plunged into as a teenager—the
fast cars, the partying, the girls—had been his cry for attention, for help—for love from a father who had turned
away from him just when he needed him more than ever.

And now it was too late. The wall between them that
had been laid, brick by brick, in Rafaello's adolescence was
too solid to break through. His father had hardened, and so
had he. Now there was only challenge—and strife.

With the latest round just about to start.

The sound of a car approaching along the drive made
him look up from his work. He could recognise the note
of the pricey little roadster that his cousin Lucia drove. It
was always important to her to be seen in the right car,
wearing the latest clothes by the best designers, and social-
ising with the right people. Hence her burning desire for a
rich husband.

When he could hear voices out in the hallway he strolled
out, forcing himself to appear relaxed.

'Rafaello?' His father stopped short.

'Papà.' Rafaello strolled forward.

'When did you get here?' demanded Enrico di Viscenti,
visibly taken aback by his son's arrival.

'This afternoon,' replied his son laconically, and proceeded to cross to where his cousin was standing, stock
still.

'Lucia,' he said dutifully, and bent to kiss her on either
cheek. She smelt of too much perfume, and her face was
too made up, but she was a handsome female for all that—
as she well knew.

'Rafaello,' she murmured. 'Such a surprise.' Her voice

was neutral, her eyes assessing. Rafaello returned her look blandly.

'As you see, the prodigal returns,' he observed laconically. 'Have you had a pleasant day?'

'Very,' returned Lucia. 'Tio Enrico accompanied me to the launch of an art exhibition in Firenze. A new artist I enjoy.'

A polite smile grazed Rafaello's mouth. 'And does he enjoy *you*, too?' he murmured.

Lucia's face stiffened immediately. 'You offend, Rafaello!' she snapped.

He shrugged elegantly. He shouldn't bait her, he knew— but he was well aware that Lucia Foscesca took her lovers mostly from artistic circles. Young men who were likely to put up with her in exchange for the influence she could bring to bear on their careers. It was one of the—many— reasons that Rafaello refused to gratify his parent's insistence on the suitability of marriage between the cousins. Call him old-fashioned—and Lucia frequently did, with a taunting laugh that could not quite hide her annoyance— but he would prefer his bride to be less well acquainted with the opposite sex.

He stilled. The word 'bride' pulled him up short. The idea that upstairs a scrawny, unlovely, sexually undiscriminating twenty-one-year-old English girl, with a nameless, fatherless child in her arms, was actually, in the eyes of the law, his *bride* of less than twelve hours struck him as completely unbelievable. Had he really gone through with it? What he had done still felt completely unreal. Insane. Then he hardened his resolve.

Yes, he had done it—put his name and hers on a wedding certificate. He had had no other option. His hand had been forced. Angry resentment seethed through him, but he banked it down. He'd get his revenge for what his stubborn, pig-headed father had made him do—get it right now.

His father was speaking again.

'And to what, may I ask—' his father's voice sounded biting '—do we owe this unexpected honour?'

Rafaello's dark eyes glinted. 'Why, Papà, tomorrow is my thirtieth birthday. Surely you knew I would come?'

Enrico di Viscenti's eyes narrowed. 'Did I?' he countered.

His son smiled. 'And here I am—as dutiful as ever. Come,' he went on, 'join me on the terrace—I believe a little…celebration…is in order.'

He was aware of Lucia's piercing scrutiny and sudden, riveted attention, and his gaze moved from his father to meet her assessing gaze. He smiled blandly, his eyes glinting just as his father's had done.

'Lucia—you will join us, of course.'

His voice was urbane, but it signalled volumes. He watched as a slow expression of satisfaction, swiftly veiled, passed over her handsome features.

'Good,' said Rafaello, and smiled again. But beneath the smile a hard, tight band seemed to be lashing itself around his heart.

CHAPTER THREE

'WELL?' demanded Enrico, taking his seat at the ornate ironwork table at the shady end of the terrace outside the formal drawing room of the villa. 'Can it be that you have come to your senses at last?' His voice was sharp, and the gaze he rested on his son even sharper.

The hard, tight rope around Rafaello's chest lashed the knot around his chest tighter.

'Did you doubt that I would, Papà?' he replied, his voice level.

His father made a sound in his throat between a growl and a rasp. 'I know you are more obstinate and self-willed than any father deserves. It was always the way with you!'

'Well,' said Rafaello, with a temporising air, 'for once I am being the model son—'

If there was a bite in his voice, no one heard it. He went on, 'But first I would like, Papà, to confirm that if I do what you want, and marry by my thirtieth birthday, you will give me undisputed control of the company. Is that right?' Rafaello addressed his father directly, keeping his voice brisk and businesslike.

'Hah!' exclaimed his father. 'You know perfectly well it is so.'

'And you give me your word on that?'

'Of course.' He sounded affronted that he had even been asked.

Rafaello smiled inexpressively. 'In which case, Papà,' he went smoothly on, his voice bland, 'you may wish me happy—and keep to your side of the agreement.'

His father stilled, his hands gripping the arms of his

chair, unable to speak for the moment. Not so Lucia. With a breathless little laugh, she spoke.

'Rafaello, you are the most abominable man.' Her voice was full of flirtatious exasperation. 'Proposing to me in such a fashion.' She gave her tinkling laugh again. 'But I shall punish you for your lack of gallantry, be sure of that.' She turned to her prospective father-in-law. 'Tell me, Enrico,' she said with coy feminine teasing, 'how shall I punish this boorish son of yours for depriving me of my rightful wooing?'

She gave another little laugh, coquettish now, and let her gaze slip back to her husband-to-be.

There was a curious look on his face. Half-shuttered, half-revealing. He held up a hand.

'Before we go any further, I think it is time for champagne, no?'

On cue, Giuseppe appeared, bearing the requisite beverage, and as he placed the tray on the table between them Rafaello murmured something to him. The man nodded, and retired. Rafaello busied himself opening the bottle and liberally filling up the glasses and spreading them around.

Lucia gave a click of irritation. 'Giuseppe has brought one glass too many,' she said acidly. 'It is high time he took his pension!'

Rafaello presented her with her foaming narrow glass. 'When you are mistress here, you may tell him so,' he said lightly.

A small but distinct smirk of satisfaction—and anticipation—curled at her scarlet mouth. Rafaello watched it, his face still quite unreadable.

His father picked up his glass and got to his feet. 'A toast.' Satisfaction rang in his voice. He was well pleased with his son's decision to finally see reason, as was his niece. 'A toast to the new Signora di Viscenti—'

Rafaello lifted his glass. 'How kind,' he murmured. There was a slight sound in the doorway to the drawing room and he tilted his head towards it. 'And how very timely.'

The girl stood there, Giuseppe just behind her. Fierce gratification surged through Rafaello. The girl made exactly the picture he had intended. As the others at the table turned to stare at her she stood there, atrociously dressed, her hair drawn back off her plain face with an elastic band, and— best of all—an open-mouthed baby on her hip. Her expression was completely blank.

Rafaello got to his feet and drew her forward. She was as stiff and unyielding as a board, and almost stumbled. He took her hand, making sure the wedding ring was visible.

'Allow me to present,' he said, in a voice that was as bland as milk, 'my wife, Signora di Viscenti.'

For a moment, as Magda stood completely immobile, wanting the earth to swallow her, there was complete silence. Then, a second later, there was uproar.

It was the old man's voice that was the loudest. It was like a lion roaring. She could understand not a word, but the rage in it was like a hurricane pouring over her. At her side Rafaello di Viscenti, the man to whom she had been legally joined in matrimony, gripped her left hand in a vice.

Her breath was frozen in her chest. The old man—who just had to be Rafaello di Viscenti's father, for the arrogance of his head and the similarity of the features argued nothing else—was still roaring. The butler-type was looking as if he'd been hit over the head by a heavy object— and the woman sitting next to the older Signor di Viscenti was simply looking totally and completely incredulous.

For one long, timeless instant there was nothing except the roaring Italian rage of the old man, and then, in absolute terror, Benji started to howl.

Magda jerked her hand free and used it to cradle her son up against her breast, turning away, back into the lavishly elegant drawing room.

What on earth was going on? A new voice had interrupted the roaring—Rafaello's. His voice was sharper, far more biting, but just as angry. Desperately Magda got as far away as she could, clutching the sobbing Benji to her while she tried to calm him—an impossible task, given the human racket going on out on the terrace.

Suddenly her sleeve was seized. There was an overpowering smell of heavy perfume, and a voice was hissing something at her in Italian. The venom in the words, incomprehensible though they were, made Magda flinch.

'Please—' she said jerkily. 'I...I don't understand.'

The woman caught breath. Her eyes narrowed. *'Inglese?'* Then she shook Magda's arm again. 'Who are you? What are you playing at? Pretending to be Rafaello's bride.' The woman tried to seize her ring finger, as if to check its authenticity, but Magda fielded her off, turning so that her body was between the woman and Benji. He was still howling fearfully.

She tore herself away and headed for the door. Stumbling, Benji still wailing in terror, she rushed across the marble hall and hurled herself up the staircase as quickly as she could, heading back to the sanctuary of the bedroom. Only when she was safely within did she pause to draw breath.

Her first thought was for Benji. He was all but hysterical now, and calming him down took for ever. But gradually, as she sat on the bed with him on her lap, rocking gently and soothingly, his anguished sobs died away. A thumb slipped into his mouth and he began to relax at last.

Magda felt shaken to the core. She might not have understood a word of that roaring anger, but the fury had been unmistakable.

Oh, dear God, what have I let myself in for? Please, please, let me wake up and find myself at home...

But it was no dream. She was indeed here, in a Tuscan villa, married to a man whose family had gone apoplectic at the news.

If she listened, she could still hear the storm raging downstairs. It seemed to have moved in from the terrace, but it was still in full flood. Magda shrank back, clutching Benji. He felt her distress and discomfort, and started whimpering again.

Footsteps, hard and angry-sounding, echoed across the marble hall. Doors slammed several times. What sounded like paternal denunciation rang up through the floorboards. Finally, in a last flurry of raised voices, there was a heavier door slamming. It reverberated right through the house, it seemed to Magda, and then everything went quiet. A moment later there came the throaty roar of a powerful internal combustion engine, gunning fiercely and then roaring away.

Silence reined. Total silence. It was almost as unnerving as the noise.

Knowing, instinctively, that the only thing she could do was keep her head tucked well down beneath the parapet, Magda kept to her room. Gradually Benji cheered up, but it was not long before another need made itself increasingly urgently felt. He was hungry.

She rifled through her hand baggage, extracting an apple and some rusks. Benji wolfed them down, still hungry when they were all gone. For the next forty-five minutes Magda tried to mollify him, but in vain. Even juice could not sate him. He needed proper food, and milk. There was nothing for it. She would have to go and find some.

With her heart in her mouth she gingerly opened the door of her bedroom. It was dusky outside on the landing. Cautiously she went down the grand marble staircase into the deserted hall. Hoping to find Giuseppe, she went through what must be a service door into a stone-flagged corridor. A door stood ajar at the end, and she entered reluctantly. If it were just herself she'd go to bed hungry, but she could not starve poor Benji. Surely someone would take pity on him?

As she entered, she realised she was in a vast, old-fashioned kitchen. A cavernous fireplace at the far end was filled with a huge cooking range. Dominating the centre of the room, however, was an endless long wooden table. To the side, beneath an old-fashioned window, an elderly woman was vigorously scrubbing a huge copper saucepan at a stone sink.

As Magda hovered hesitantly in the doorway the woman turned to stare at her.

'*Si?*' she demanded, in an unfriendly tone. Her face was strong-boned, and her expression was anything but welcoming. She glared at Magda.

Magda swallowed. '*Mi dispiace,*' she ventured haltingly, hoping she was pronouncing it right from the Italian phrasebook she had bought. '*Ma…este possible…?*'

'I speak English,' the woman snapped at her. 'What is it you want?'

Almost, Magda turned and ran. Then, as Benji huddled in closer to her, sensing her unease, she swallowed again. 'I am so sorry—' her voice was almost a whisper '—but would it be possible, please…a little food…and some milk…for my baby…?'

Fierce black eyes from beneath beetling greying brows bored into her. She felt her throat tighten with tension. Surely the woman would not refuse sustenance for a little child, however angry she was at having been disturbed—as she so clearly was—by such an unwelcome person as the female whom Rafaello di Viscenti had brought here to cause uproar.

The eyes were scanning her, taking in her shabby clothes, her thin, drab figure, the baby clutching her, and then going back to Magda's strained, nervous face. Suddenly the woman's expression changed. She threw up her hands, exclaiming something vociferously in her native language, and bustled forward.

'Come—come—come…' she announced. 'Sit—' She propelled Magda with surprisingly strong arms, considering her age, and plumped her down at one of the chairs at the long table. 'You are hungry, yes? Foolish girl—why did you not ring from your room?'

'I…I…didn't want to be a nuisance…' Magda stammered.

The woman made a tch-ing noise in her throat. 'A baby must not wait for his food,' she announced. 'Nor the mother.'

She bustled off to the far end of the kitchen, this time to the cooking range. There were various pots on it, and out of one she proceeded to scoop up, with the aid of a huge wooden implement like a spoon, with horizontal prongs, a generous serving of spaghetti. On top of this she ladled spoonfuls of tomato sauce. She carried the dish back to Magda, placed it on the table, and deftly tied a huge teatowel around Benji's neck to protect his clothes from the sauce.

Benji's little mouth was already wide open, and Magda had scarcely time to check the pasta was not too hot before he had seized her wrist and was guiding the forkful towards him.

He made a hearty meal, and as soon as he had finished another, even larger bowl of pasta and sauce was placed in front of Magda.

'Eat,' the woman instructed, taking Benji from her. Balancing him expertly on her own hip, she turned to fill a cup with some water, and gave it to him to drink from with equal expertise. Surprisingly, Benji seemed perfectly happy with this, and started to gurgle.

The woman beamed, and addressed him in voluble Italian of which Magda caught only one word—*bambino*. Then, extracting a wooden stirrer from a large earthenware

pot on the window ledge, the woman presented it to
Benji—who grabbed it eagerly—and sat herself down opposite Magda.

'Eat,' she repeated, as Magda paused in her own con-
sumption of pasta. It was totally delicious, and she was
wolfing it down as eagerly as Benji had.

'Thank you,' she murmured, still feeling intensely awkward as well as grateful.

The woman let her finish, amusing herself by entertain-
ing Benji, who was in no way dismayed to be addressed in
a foreign language. Magda watched covertly, between
mouthfuls. The woman was obviously very experienced
with children, and knew exactly what Benji found enter-
taining—which was largely banging the wooden stirrer on
the table and trying to knock over the pepperpot.

Magda scraped the last of the tomato sauce with her
spoon and gave a satisfied sigh. The woman looked across
at her.

'So,' she announced. 'Now we talk.' She hefted Benji
from one side of her lap to the other. 'You tell me,' she
said in her heavily accented English. 'Is Rafaello the father?'

A look of total stupefaction filled Magda's face. Her
mouth fell open in shock. Her reaction seemed to please
the woman.

'Well, that is one relief at least,' she announced. The
snap was back in her voice, and Magda, finally over-
wrought by all the events of the day, found her throat tightening.

'So,' went on the woman relentlessly, 'he has married
simply to make his father angry. *Idiota!*'

Magda stared helplessly. She didn't know what to say.
Didn't know what she *could* say. She had had no idea that
she would be walking into such a volatile situation. But
evidently it did not surprise the housekeeper—or so she
assumed this woman must be.

'Is he mad, finally to do this to his father?' the woman exclaimed. 'Always the same—always. Always they fight like…like the men of sheep…their heads—so!' She slid one hand past Benji and made a fist, together with the other, and clashed the knuckles together, like rams' horns impacting. 'But this—this is the worst.'

'I…I'm sorry,' said Magda. It seemed the only thing to say.

The woman said something in Italian. 'Well, well,' she went on in English. 'It is done now. So, if Rafaello is not the father of your child, why do you marry him?'

The bluntness of the question took Magda aback.

'Um—Signor di Viscenti said he needed to be married for legal reasons by his thirtieth birthday. I…I agreed because…'

She felt silent. Suddenly it seemed shameful to admit that she had married a complete stranger for financial gain.

The woman's eyes took on a shrewd expression.

'He offers you money, yes?'

Colour stained Magda's cheekbones. She looked down. 'With…with the money Signor di Viscenti has promised me I can buy a little house for my son.'

The tch-ing noise came again. 'And the father of your *bambino*? No, no, do not tell me.' The voice sounded old and tired. 'He has gone, no? It is always the same—the men do not care and the girls are foolish.'

She started to clear away the empty pasta dishes, handing Benji back to Magda. 'Well, well, there is nothing to be done. But I tell you—' a dark, warning look came Magda's way '—after this his father will never forgive Rafaello.'

Sunlight pressing on Rafaello's eyes made him groan. Slowly, he roused to an unwelcome consciousness, and then wished himself still in oblivion. He'd stormed out of the villa yesterday evening, his father's curses still ringing in his ears. Tearing down the valley in his high-powered sports car, he'd replayed every ugly word that had been exchanged. His father's incandescent rage and his own vicious taunting, telling him that thanks to his insistence on his son marrying he now had a daughter-in-law who came complete with a fatherless baby and who cleaned toilets for a living.

For ten seconds he'd thought Enrico would have a cardiac arrest on the spot—until his temper had burst out again and he'd rained down verbal abuse on his son for shaming the family name. As for Lucia, she'd been wearing an expression like Lucretia Borgia on a bad hair day—looking for someone to poison that could only be him.

He'd ended the night working his way through a bottle of grappa and damning the whole world.

A punishing shower brought him back to a semblance of half-life. It was nearly noon, a glance at his watch told him. Noon on his thirtieth birthday. He didn't feel like celebrating. He crossed to the window of his bedroom and stared out balefully. Below, the vista of the gardens brought him no comfort. He tried to focus on important things. He must go to Rome and call a board meeting to confirm him as the new chairman, then start implementing the strategy for global expansion into the USA and Australia for Viscenti AG that he'd been planning for so long.

A movement to the side of his field of vision caught his eye. The girl and her little boy were rounding the side of the house. She was going very slowly, holding his hand as he toddled unsteadily along the gravelled path. *Dio*, he'd all but forgotten about her. He watched her stoop swiftly to catch the child as he stumbled momentarily and then set him back on course.

What the hell was he going to do about her? She'd served her purpose—provided him with the wife he required to confront his father. He didn't need her any more, but he could not risk giving rise to public speculation that his was a fraudulent marriage by sending her back to England straight away. He gave a shrug and turned away. He would tell Maria to keep her out of his hair and she could enjoy a free holiday at the villa while he was in Rome.

He was just about to turn away when another figure came into view, stalking out from the house.

Lucia.

She was clearly on course to the girl, and in a raging temper.

Out in the gardens, Magda came to a halt. That woman, whoever she was, who had been as furious at Rafaello's announcement as his father had been, was heading purposefully towards her. Magda waited apprehensively. The woman's high heels scrunched noisily on the path.

She came to a stop in front of her. Yesterday Magda had been in too much shock to take in anything about the woman. Now she could see she was an immaculately coiffed, flashing-eyed brunette, wearing a tight-fitting designer outfit.

Her eyes were narrowed with blazing hostility. Magda's hand tightened over Benji, who was crouching down to inspect the gravel.

Whatever the woman was going to say to her remained unsaid. More crunching footsteps sounded, heavier and rapid, and Rafaello appeared around the corner of the house. He was wearing, this summer morning, a lightweight suit in pale grey, and he looked, as Magda stared helplessly, completely breathtaking.

He launched into rapid Italian directed at Lucia.

'You should leave, Lucia. There is nothing for you here—there never was. You should have known I would never marry you.'

Lucia's eyes flashed angrily. Her face contorted. 'So you married this *putana* instead of me! Look at her. She's like some scrawny chicken.'

The contempt in the woman's eyes as she raked Magda's face made Rafaello's jaw tighten.

'Basta.' He cast a rapid glance at the girl. She was looking ashen suddenly, and for a moment Rafaello hoped she didn't have the wit to realise what Lucia had called her. But doubtless she could hear the hostility in his cousin's voice, whatever language she spoke. He took a sharp breath.

'I think, Lucia, it would be best if you returned to your apartment in Firenze. You have done my father no favours in making him think of you as a prospective daughter-in-law.'

An ugly look flashed in the woman's dark eyes. 'And you think you have done him a favour bringing him home that…that girl?' she spat angrily. 'I hope you are proud of what you have done, Rafaello.'

She turned on her stilettos and stalked off. Slowly, Magda let out her breath, unaware till now that she'd been holding it. Benji was clinging to her hand, huddled close, clearly frightened by the anger all around him.

'It's all right, muffin,' she whispered comfortingly into his hair, as she scooped him up into her arms.

But it wasn't all right. It was all wrong. Everything here in this beautiful place was as wrong as it could be. Her throat tightened.

'You should have told me.'

Where the words came from she did not know. Where the courage to say them came from she certainly didn't know. But she had said them, and now she was looking at the man she had thought she was marrying simply for a matter of legal detail in reasons of business.

But this was surely nothing to do with Viscenti AG—it couldn't be! The anger and fury that had erupted since she had stepped out on to the terrace yesterday could not possibly be about something as impersonal as business.

This was family. Ugly, emotional, volatile, bitter family.

'Told you what?'

Rafaello's voice was sharper than he meant. His unpleasant exchange with Lucia made it sound harsher.

'Told me that I was walking into a human minefield,' Magda said tightly. 'Everyone is furious that you married me. Your father, that woman—whoever she is—even the housekeeper and your butler. I didn't know everyone here would be angry with me.' There was a tremor in her voice she tried desperately to conceal.

'They are not angry with you,' Rafaello answered flatly. 'They are angry with me. And the only person I am angry with,' he continued, even more flatly, 'is my father. You might as well know…' He took a heavy breath. 'He wanted me to marry Lucia—she is my cousin, and would like to be Signora di Viscenti and have my money to spend. She worked on him to persuade him she would be the ideal wife for me—and the ideal mother of the grandchildren he is obsessed with having. He sought to force my compliance by threatening to sell his controlling share of the family company. That I will not permit—I have worked too hard for the last ten years to throw away all my efforts just to ensure I am not manipulated into marriage with a woman I do not wish to marry. So I outmanoeuvred him. I arrived the day before my thirtieth birthday already—already married.'

'To a *putana*.' Her voice was even flatter than his.

Rafaello stiffened. Could she possibly know what that word meant? As if she could read his thoughts, she said thinly, 'A whore—isn't that the right translation, Mr di Viscenti?'

She started to walk past him. She just wanted to get away. The ugliness around her was choking her.

He caught her arm. 'You must take no notice of Lucia. She is bitter and angry. She lashed out at you. That is all.'

'Thank you—but I prefer not to be lashed out at in the

first place. You and your cousin know nothing of me or my circumstances—or my son's.'

His face darkened at her retort. 'I know that a young girl with a baby and no man to support it means that you were, at the very least, careless about who you chose to sleep with.'

Her expression stiffened. 'I think I was more careless, Mr di Viscenti, about whom I chose to marry yesterday morning. I definitely should have checked out your charming relations.'

She shook her arm free and walked rapidly away from him. Behind her, Rafaello swore. Then, quickening his step, he caught up with her.

'I regret that you were exposed to such a scene,' he said tightly. 'But I would suggest you remember that you are being paid a substantial amount of money to undertake what you have done.'

She stopped, deflating instantly at his blunt reminder. She stared down at his polished shoes. He was right—and she must not forget it, however economical with the truth he had been about his reasons for marrying her.

'I've done my best, Mr di Viscenti,' she answered with quiet dignity, lifting her eyes to him. 'I've done what you wanted me to do, when you wanted me to do it. But I really didn't appreciate that one of my duties would be to serve as a punch-bag for those of your household who are displeased by your marriage.'

Rafaello's lip curled. 'Are you asking for more money?'

Her face seemed to whiten under his question. 'No, Mr di Viscenti, I am not asking for more money. I am asking merely not to be subject to the anger and insults of members of your household. If nothing else, it is upsetting for Benji. And now, if you please, if you would be so kind as to give me my instructions for the day I shall carry them out to the best of my ability. Do you wish me to return to my room?'

'You may do whatever you please.' A spurt of quite unnatural anger at her response shot through him. 'The house and grounds are at your disposal. I am not an ogre— and I have expressed my regret for my cousin's behaviour. She will be leaving shortly, as shall I. Please make yourself at home.'

He walked away, leaving Magda feeling impotently angry. Slowly the feeling drained away. What was the point of her making a fuss like that? The rich were heedlessly indifferent to others; she knew that well enough. To Rafaello di Viscenti she was nothing more than a tool to be used—hired and paid for. When she was of no use to him she should stay quiet and not make a fuss—whatever uproar was going on around her.

She let Benji slip down to the ground again, and silently watched him busying himself scooping up handfuls of gravel and throwing them down again with a satisfied air. When, finally, he was bored, she took his hand.

'Come on, let's go back indoors.'

She made her way around the side of the villa, back to the servants' entrance at the rear. At least here she felt more at ease. The housekeeper—whose name, she had been informed over breakfast, when she had tentatively made her way down to the kitchen once Benji had surfaced, was Maria—at least seemed to have decided to tolerate her. She was being kind enough, in a sort of rough-edged way that Magda suspected was her customary manner, hiding a very soft heart.

'Milk,' pronounced Maria now, as Magda entered the huge kitchen, 'for the *bambino*.'

Benji toddled cheerfully over to her, expressing confidence in being welcomed by this new person in his life that was amply repaid. Chatting away to him in Italian, Maria sat him on the table and presented him with a mug of creamy milk.

'*Latte,*' she informed the infant as he gulped down the contents greedily, and repeated the word several times.

'La',' replied Benji, and beamed at her expectantly. 'Mo'?'

'He means more,' said Magda diffidently. 'Um—*piu*?' she ventured, racking her brain for what she had read in her Italian phrasebook.

'*Ancora,*' corrected Maria, refilling Benji's mug. She looked at Magda. 'He is a good boy. Even with no father.' Her black eyes rested on Magda, and then softened. 'But you love your *bambino*, that I can see. And that makes you a good woman.'

Unaccountably, the rough kindness made Magda's eyes prick with tears. The housekeeper made her tch-ing sound, and placed another mug of creamy milk in front of her, as well as refilling Benji's.

'Drink,' she said again, to both of them.

To her surprise, Magda found the rest of the day actually enjoyable. Maria took her under her wing, managing to find time to make a great fuss of Benji, which he openly adored. Fetching his toys from her room, Magda settled in the vast kitchen at one end of the table while Maria got on with the task of serving lunch—presumably for Rafaello's father. Lucia had, according to a terse announcement by Giuseppe as he looked into the kitchen at some point, departed. Judging from the way she was spoken about, Magda gathered that Rafaello's cousin was no favourite below stairs. Rafaello, too, had gone, roaring off in his car, the noise of his departure causing Maria's lips to tighten ominously. Magda, however, could only be relieved.

It was much easier being here in the servants' quarters. After all, she reasoned, it was where she naturally belonged.

After lunch came a real treat. Maria took her and Benji out to the swimming pool. Set in a sheltered walled garden, the water shimmered invitingly in the sunshine. Benji, who adored swimming, tottered eagerly towards it.

'Won't Signor di Viscenti mind?' Magda asked diffidently.

Maria's mouth tightened. 'You are Signora di Viscenti. No, no, do not tell me that it is in name only. He has married you. You are his wife. If you wish to swim— swim.'

Magda could not resist. Although the water was still a little chilly, Benji splashed so vigorously and enthusiastically in the rubber ring and water wings that Magda had no fears he would take cold. In the peaceful sunshine, with the pool to themselves, the time flashed by.

Afterwards, exhausted by his exertions, Benji fell fast asleep on a lounger beneath the shade of a large umbrella that Giuseppe had opened for them at the poolside. At his side, Magda sunned herself.

Whatever the storms raging around her, one thing was for sure: she would never again in her life get the chance to enjoy such idyllic surroundings. She would make the most of what was happening to her, she resolved, and let everything else wash over her head. Rafaello di Viscenti's quarrels were nothing to do with her.

She spent a quiet evening with Benji, keeping Maria and Giuseppe company in the kitchen. No one sent for her, and Rafaello did not return to the villa.

'He has gone to Rome,' said Maria. She sounded disapproving. Magda simply felt relieved.

Later, with Benji asleep in the huge bed, she sat beside him, sipping the coffee Maria brought up, reading for an hour or two. Just before she turned in herself she sat by the open window, drinking in the soft sounds of the Italian night.

My second night in Italy. It seemed hardly possible, yet it was so. As she looked out into the velvet darkness, the noise and tatty raucousness of South London seemed a universe away.

I am fortunate beyond my dreams, she said softly to herself. *Simply to have this experience is more than I ever thought I could have.*

A face swam into her vision. Dark-eyed, olive-skinned, high cheekbones, sculpted mouth...male beauty in its ultimate form. She felt her heart give a crazy, unstoppable little skip. Oh, he was indeed the kind of man you could feel weak at the knees over.

Weak in the heart over!

But Rafaello di Viscenti was as remote from her as if he were a portrait by Titian hanging on a *palazzo* wall.

Her lips pressed together and she stared out, eyes wide and painful, into the Tuscan night, where the wind winnowed softly in the cypress trees and the scent of flowers exhaled like the sweet breath of the sleeping earth.

Slowly, she got to her feet and went to bed.

CHAPTER FOUR

RAFAELLO gunned his sports car and overtook a hopelessly slow tourist hire-car travelling along the Pisa-Firenze autostrada well below the maximum speed limit. He should be in a good mood. Viscenti AG was his completely, all confining paternal strings cut. But he was not. He did not want another encounter with his father—still less with the girl he had made his bride.

She made him feel uncomfortable.

There was no reason for it, he told himself impatiently, gunning the engine again. He was setting her up financially for life. She had nothing to complain of.

Except being dumped in a strange place with not a word of the language and having everyone yelling their heads off all around her...

His mouth tightened, and he changed gears more roughly than the superb engine warranted.

And you walking out on her and leaving her to it.

He overtook another car and cruised back into his lane. Well, of course he'd not hung around pointlessly at the villa! How could he have? The whole purpose of this total farce was to call his father's bluff so he could get Lucia off his case and not lose his life's work at Viscenti AG. He wasn't there to nursemaid one of life's waifs and strays just because he'd happened to marry her the day before. She knew what she was doing when she signed the papers.

No, she didn't...

The irritating voice in his head nagged at him again, making him blast his horn at a car hogging the outside lane.

Just like she told you—she didn't know she was going to

detonate an explosion of family fury. She walked into it and hadn't a clue.

Yes, well, he thought grimly, there was still no reason for him to feel bad about it. She was just some not-too-bright London girl who'd probably got pregnant on purpose to live on social security—she couldn't have understood a word of what was being yelled about yesterday. And today she'd had the run of a millionaire's villa—a free holiday in the sun. His father wouldn't go near her, he knew—he would simply lock himself in the library and fume—Lucia had been sent off-pitch, and he'd made sure that Giuseppe and Maria would keep an eye on the girl and her kid.

Ruthlessly he quashed any riposte to this final analysis of the situation and put his foot down hard on the accelerator. The powerful car shot forward and Rafaello felt a rush of familiar exhilaration.

Speed always put his troubles far behind him.

They caught up with him again, though, when he drew to a halt in front of the garage at the rear of the villa some half an hour later. A familiar car met his eyes. Wonderful, he thought grimly. Reinforcements had been summoned.

He should not have been surprised. His father always turned to his sister when he wanted to complain about his son. Well, Tia Elizavetta could say what she liked on this one—and she would too; she had a sharp tongue in her head—but it was too late for recriminations. He had out-manoeuvred his father and that was that.

Giuseppe intercepted him the moment he stepped inside the hallway. He was looking poker-faced and Rafaello knew he was not pleased—the moment the man opened his mouth he knew who he wasn't pleased with.

It was 'Signor' this and 'Signor' that, uttered in such stiff accents that Rafaello got the message loud and clear. He was in the doghouse with both Giuseppe and the formidable Maria.

'My aunt and uncle are here, I see,' he said, doing his best to ignore the glacial attitude of this man who knew him better than his own father.

'*Si, signor.* They arrived an hour ago. They are with your father.'

There was a wealth of meaning in his words. Rafaello nodded. 'Well, I might as well get it over and done with,' he remarked. 'Are they in the library?'

Giuseppe indicated that they were.

'Right,' said Rafaello, and started to head towards the double doors leading through to the library.

- A reproving cough came from behind him. He halted, and turned his head questioningly.

'Signora di Viscenti is in the gardens with her little boy,' Giuseppe informed him, his face studiedly expressionless. 'Perhaps you would like to greet her before seeing your aunt and uncle?'

Rafaello stilled. 'Later,' was all he said, and headed into the library. Behind him, Giuseppe's disapproval was tangible.

As he walked into the long room he could tell instantly that his father had been enumerating his son's crimes and misdemeanours in graphic detail. His aunt had her older-sister look about her, and his uncle had the familiar glazed look that meant his mind was miles away from yet another family furore.

'So! You deign to return at last,' was his father's opening salvo as his son approached. 'First you destroy me, and then you desert me. But what other treatment should I expect from you, hah?'

Rafaello felt the familiar surge of tense exasperation fill him. 'I needed to go to Rome, Papà. I had to call a board meeting as soon as possible to confirm the new chairmanship.'

A hiss that sounded like a steam train escaped his father's mouth. 'Already. Already you discard me. Well, when you leave the family company in ruins with your reckless over-ambition remember that you took it from me by treachery.'

'You gave me your word, Papà, to let me run the company if I were married by my thirtieth birthday. That condition I have met. That is all.' Rafaello spoke with iron control, and watched the colour mount dangerously in his father's face. His own darkened, and his control slipped fatally. 'I am not a schoolboy any longer. What you attempted to do was unforgivable. This is my life—you have no right to play with it like a toy.'

His voice had risen, and so had his temper.

His aunt stepped forward, holding up her hands between them.

'Rafaello, enough. And you, too, Enrico. Can you at least try for civility if nothing else?'

'*Civility?*' Enrico spat. 'You ask for civility, Elizavetta? After what he has done?'

His sister gave a heavy sigh. 'It astonishes me, Enrico, that after all these years you still do not know Rafaello is as stubborn as you. Good God, where else does he get it from but you? You tried to force his hand—and he retaliated. What did you expect him to do, with your blood in him? I warned you not to pursue your stubborn course! If he had wanted to marry Lucia he would have done so without your help.'

Her brother looked mutinous at this criticism, but his sister gave him no chance to respond. She turned her attention to her nephew.

'And thank heaven you had more sense than to marry Lucia. One day, I hope—' her voice had a reproving note for Rafaello '—you will make a marriage based on love. But first you have to disentangle yourself from this ridiculous misalliance you have tied yourself up with. I do not approve of what you have done, Rafaello, I tell you that straight. However,' she went on imperiously, 'I still have hopes that you might yet prove yourself something more than a business brain and a handsome face.' Her voice became sharper than ever. 'You might even bring yourself to greet your aunt.'

She held her arms out commandingly, and Rafaello crossed to bestow the customary kiss and greeting on either cheek.

'Yes,' she said tartly to him. 'That is better.'

She held his eye a moment. For all her sharp tongue he got on well with his outspoken aunt. 'You and I will talk, young man,' she told him. 'And I will contrive, not for the first time and no doubt not for the last,' she said wearily, 'to see if I can sort out this latest disaster.' She let him go and stood back. 'But first I should like to refresh myself. The journey from Bologna was tiring. Your uncle has been working too hard—his lecture tour was arduous and he has papers to write. You should time these tempests better. Bernardo—come.'

Sweeping her husband with her, barely giving him time to exchange hurried greetings with his nephew by marriage, she headed for the door. For a moment Rafaello stood uncertainly, looking across at his father, still smouldering like a keg of dynamite threatening to explode. Why? he thought bitterly. Why is it always, always, *always* such a battle?

A wave of depression swept over him. His father was a stranger. An angry stranger.

A fierce light sparked in Enrico's eyes as he saw his son looking at him. 'And you—you can get out, too. Get out of my sight.'

Rafaello did not need telling twice. He turned on his heel and left.

A swim, he thought. That was what he needed. The weather was warming up, and the physical exertion would do him good. Drain off some of that hard, angry emotion roiling around inside him like bilgewater in a rotting hull. But when, clad in his swimming trunks, towel over his shoulder, he strode through the stone archway that led into the walled pool area, he stopped dead.

There was someone in the pool already. In fact, he realised instantly, two people. His bride and her son.

He watched them for a moment, half hidden by some cascading climbing roses. She was playing with the child, standing in the shallow end, legs apart, throwing the infant up into the air with a whooshing noise and catching him as he plunged back down into the water. She was laughing, and so was the child—uproariously. Evidently this experience was of enormous pleasure to him, for the little boy gave a shout of glee as he went up into the air before descending yet again for a mighty splash.

Rafaello stepped forward and immediately Magda halted in mid-lift, seeing him enter the pool area. She froze, indifferent to the abrupt wail of the baby as his fun was interrupted.

She was staring at him—horror-struck, so it seemed to Rafaello, and he felt an immediate burst of irritation. There was no need to look at him as if he were Dracula. But she was already wading to the semicircle of steps that led out of the water as fast as she could, wielding the protesting baby in front of her like a shield. She started to climb out hastily.

'I'm very sorry. I didn't realise I should not be swimming now,' she said apologetically, and Rafaello experienced another stab of exasperation. He felt like Frankenstein's monster as well as Dracula.

'There is no need to get out,' he informed her, dropping his towel down on to one of the loungers. 'I only require one lane. Continue with the child.'

But she was getting out of the pool all the same. 'No, no—we've finished.'

Judging by the wail that the child let out at that point, he, for one, considered his swim far from finished.

'Stay in the water.'

His voice came out harsher than he meant it to. It was just that there was no reason for the girl to be looking at him like that. As if he were an ogre.

'No, really…' the girl mumbled. She'd stopped staring at him. Her gaze seemed awkward now instead, and she started to sidle towards the lounger her things were on, holding the protesting baby under his armpits. His legs kicked out furiously. His wet body started to slip through her hands, and for a moment Rafaello thought he would slide through them. He lunged forward just as the girl, at the same time, bent her knees to lower the child from a safer height to the ground.

For the barest second his eyes met hers, before he backed away, realising his assistance was unnecessary. What he saw in their expression shocked him. She looked absolutely terrified.

He straightened up. 'I thought he was going to fall,' he said.

She straightened as well, keeping hold of the baby's hand, though he was tugging as hard as he could in the direction of the water.

'His name is Benji,' she said suddenly, and just as quickly she wasn't looking terrified at all. She was looking fierce. 'Just because he doesn't have a father doesn't mean he doesn't have a name.'

Rafaello's mouth tightened. She was a pint-sized thing, he thought. The swimsuit she was wearing should have been thrown away long ago. Thinking about it, it probably had been. It was a size too large for her, for a start, and its elasticity was completely gone. It was crinkling around her abdomen and hips, bunching over her squashed, unappealing breasts. It was also a hideous shade of purple and green, in a spectacularly unlovely pattern.

As he looked at it in disgust he realised her expression had changed again. It was one he recognised. She'd worn a similar expression the time he'd looked her over in his flat, deciding that she was ideal for his purposes. This time he recognised it.

Mortification.

He also recognised his own reaction to it—that same sense of discomfort he'd felt on the drive back from the airport this evening. OK, he admitted, so it wasn't the poor girl's fault she looked about as appealing as a plucked chicken. And she certainly didn't have any spare cash to splash out on a decent swimsuit that might actually do something *for* her body instead of *against* it. In fact, that restriction must apply to her whole wardrobe, which was certainly the most appalling he'd ever encountered.

A sudden image of Lucia flashed into his mind, curved and poured into her endless designer numbers, worn a bare handful of times before being discarded.

The comparison was unkind. The girl in front of him might have come from a different planet.

He frowned. Another memory flashed in his mind— Lucia calling her a *putana*.

The stab of discomfort came again, stronger this time. What the hell business had Lucia to call her that? The idea was ludicrous.

More than ludicrous.

It was offensive.

His eyes flicked to the child again, still desperate to get back into the pool. OK, so there was no father around— but accusing her of being feckless, as she obviously had been, was hardly the same as accusing her of prostitution.

You know nothing of me or my circumstances…

Her accusation of the morning bit into his mind. And she'd understood what Lucia had called her. She shouldn't have, but she had.

The feeling of discomfort mounted.

She was dragging the wailing boy towards the lounger, speaking to him sternly, and had managed to get a towel around his little body. He promptly threw it off with an even louder wail. But the girl wrapped him up in it yet again, and just as swiftly wrapped herself as well, knotting the towel around her like a sarong. She straightened up.

Maybe it was because the towel veiled from his eyes the hideous swimsuit, or maybe it was the lowering sun casting an amber glow over the pool area, reflecting warm light on to her, but suddenly he thought she looked quite graceful, with her slender limbs and sunlit skin. She had long hair, he noticed with mild surprise. It wasn't loose, though, it was tied back in a long stringy ponytail. He hadn't even realised she did have long hair—she'd always had it clamped on the back of her head by some kind of clip in a totally style-less way.

He watched her pick up the kiddie, hoist him on to her hip. His wails had died away now, and he was staring at Rafaello instead, with his big dark eyes. What had she said his name was? Benji? He'd try and remember next time. It might stop her correcting him in that snippy way.

She cleared up her stuff and left, muttering a defiant 'Excuse me' as she moved past with all her clutter. The child—*Benji*, he reprimanded himself—was clutching his inflatable ring as if it were golden treasure.

A mixture of exasperation and discomfort filled Rafaello. The girl had obviously been enjoying herself with her baby—*Benji*, he reminded himself—and now they were hurrying away. It was quite unnecessary. They wouldn't have bothered him, provided they stayed out of his swimming lane.

Well, too late now. She'd insisted on going. It was hardly his fault, he told himself, feeling irritated. He took up a position by the edge of the pool and executed a perfect racing dive, ploughing down to the far end twenty metres away in a punishing, rapid freestyle.

Forty minutes and two kilometres later he hauled himself out, tired but in a markedly better mood. The sun had gone now, and dusk was settling in, but the air was still pleasantly warm. He walked down the length of the pool, picked up his towel and rubbed his hair, before wrapping the towel over his body.

Hunger nipped at him. He'd shower, change and take an aperitif. His aunt would pounce on him, he knew, and give him an earful, but his mood after exercise was good enough to put up with it. He was glad she'd turned up. She always managed to calm his father down—she'd been doing it all her life.

And having his aunt and uncle present would certainly help to make dinner less of an ordeal. They would help to keep things civil. He'd try and get Bernardo started on whatever his current research was—his uncle didn't speak much, except when it was on his favourite scholarly topic. Then he could expound for ever if he found a willing victim.

A smile curved Rafaello's mouth as he headed back indoors. He had a lot of time for Bernardo—there was a whole lot of good sense in there, and a tempering disposition that went well with his aunt's acid-tongued approach to life—and family. They'd never had children, and Rafaello had fond memories of both his aunt and uncle making a huge fuss of him when he'd been little, arriving for family celebrations and holidays up in the cool Tuscan hills.

Right on cue, some twenty minutes later, as he sipped his chilled beer, sitting out on the terrace overlooking the gardens stretching away all around the villa, the cypress trees framing the vista of the valley below, he heard the businesslike tread of his aunt approaching. He stood up as she came to him, and helped her take a seat.

'So,' she began, with a martial light in her eye, 'now we talk.'

Upstairs, Magda was giving Benji his bath. It was hardly necessary—he was as clean as a whistle from the pool—

but it seemed compensation for him after having been dragged away from the water. She didn't feel too bad about it, however—it hadn't been their first dip. They'd already swum twice earlier in the day, which had been spent, like yesterday, in blissful ease.

She'd swum, had lunch with Maria and Giuseppe, swum again, napped with Benji and then explored the beautiful gardens and grounds of the villa—a skilful mix of formality and cultivated wildness—even venturing further up the hill behind into the lower slopes of the plentiful chestnut woods that stretched behind the villa. Hearing from Maria on their return that Rafaello's aunt and uncle had arrived, she'd hidden herself and Benji in the pool area again for a final swim.

She cringed inwardly with memory. Oh, why hadn't she left the pool ten minutes earlier instead of being caught by Rafaello? If embarrassment was fatal she'd have been dead on the spot! For the millionth time his image burned into her retinas—six feet of honed, smooth, tanned muscle, total physical male perfection...

Thank God she hadn't blushed. That would have been the ultimate mortification—letting him see that she couldn't take her eyes from him. As it was she had simply had the familiar mortification—if more intense this time—of having him look at her as if she were covered in slime.

She sat back on her heels, letting Benji scoop up a handful of foam and plaster it to the tiles beside the bath with a gurgling laugh. She pushed back a strand of unruly hair that had got loose, and as she twisted her head slightly she caught sight of herself in the wall-length mirror inset opposite the bath.

Oh, God, she looked so awful. Her T-shirt was totally shapeless and faded. Not that anything could have flattered her, she knew. Her face was unremarkable, her hair dull and mousy, besides being stringy and overlong. She tried to remember the last time she'd had it cut and failed—long hair was cheaper than short hair.

She was a mess, repellent to any man—let alone a man so blessed with gorgeousness as Rafaello di Viscenti. The memory of him staring disparagingly at her, his long-lashed eyes sweeping condemningly over her every unpleasing feature, made her feel ashamed.

She knew such a feeling was illogical. It was not her fault she was plain, nor Rafaello's that he was male beauty incarnate. Nor, she added punishingly, was it his fault that any woman who caught his eye would have to be a stunning beauty for him to appreciate her.

A dab of flying foam caught her on the chin, distracting her. Benji chuckled wickedly. Magda's frown lightened, and deliberately she put aside all painful thoughts. Benji could not care less what she looked like—all he wanted was her love. And that—she smiled down lovingly at him, and paddled more foam in his direction—he had for ever and ever.

Afterwards—bathroom tidied and Benji changed into a clean nappy and his second-hand pyjamas—she sat him in the middle of the bed, propped up against the pillows with his scruffy but adored little teddy bear, and settled down to read his favourite bedtime picture book. He was tired tonight, and would soon be asleep, she could see. When he was she would sneak down to the kitchen and beg a sandwich for her own supper—with guests in the house she did not want to be a nuisance to Maria and Giuseppe. And she would feel much safer tucked up away in her bedroom, out of sight of any of Rafaello's family—and especially Rafaello.

It would be what he wanted, too, she knew.

Rafaello had not expected to enjoy his aunt's lecture, and he did not. But at least she could see his side of things as well—unlike his father—even though she told him roundly that the pair of them deserved everything they handed out to each other.

'You are impossible, the pair of you!' she finished. Then, taking another breath, she said, 'Very well, now that I have made that plain to you, you had best go and fetch this bride of yours.'

Rafaello stalled in the act of lifting his beer glass to his mouth. He'd been nursing it all the way through the lecture and he was now in need of its reviving contents. He stared at his aunt.

'Well, there is no point hiding her any longer. I might as well see for myself,' his aunt told him.

'She is in her room,' Rafaello said stiffly.

'Well, go and fetch her. She can't stay up there all night.'

Rafaello set down his glass with a distinct click. 'She is looking after her child,' he said remotely.

His aunt waved her hand in an Italian fashion. 'One of the maids can sit with the infant. You had better go and see if she is ready to come down to dine yet. You know your father cannot abide tardiness.'

Rafaello's jaw tightened. 'You do not quite understand, Tia—' he began, but his aunt cut him short.

'What I understand, Rafaello,' she said, and there was a definite snap in her voice, 'is that you deserted the poor girl the moment you brought her here. Haring off to Rome, if you please, simply because you are obsessed with that wretched company. But I tell you this: however pressing your business affairs—however eager you are to take over from Enrico—you do *not* abandon your bride in your own home. It is insupportable. And I do not care *how* much of a marriage of convenience it is to you, or how much of a misalliance. There are decencies to be observed and this is one of them. Whoever the girl is, however utterly unsuitable she is to be Signora di Viscenti, you have married her and that is that. She is your wife.'

Rafaello lips pressed together. This was not something

he had anticipated at all! He stood up abruptly, looking down into his aunt's militant expression.

'Very well,' he said bitingly, and then suddenly found himself continuing, 'But I must ask you to…to go easy on her.'

It was that stab of discomfort again, pricking at him. His aunt was a formidable woman—she would make mincemeat of that hapless creature upstairs in her bedroom. And suddenly he found that the thought of the girl ripped to shreds by his aunt's sharp tongue was painful.

But as he spoke he found his aunt was looking at him with a strange light in her eye. As if he had surprised her.

'I shall take into account her…unfortunate circumstances,' she answered dryly. 'Despite my brother's histrionics as to her morals and background, from what Maria tells me—yes, I have had a talk with her as well, and very enlightening it was, too!—the girl is nothing more than a misfortunate single mother, of which a large number abound these days. She certainly seems to have convinced Maria she is nothing worse, and that is no easy task. I admit I am curious to see her for myself. Well, be off with you. Go and fetch your wife.'

His wife. As Rafaello strode away at his aunt's imperious bidding, the words tolled in his brain. This was not supposed to be happening. The girl was not supposed to intrude into his life in this way—simply marrying her had been intrusion enough. And now here was his aunt, demanding that he fetch her as if she were his wife for real.

But she is your wife—you married her.

But I didn't intend to get landed with her, he thought balefully as he took the stairs two at a time. He reached the door of her bedroom and rapped sharply.

Magda started. She'd been half dozing, watching the foolish moths fly in through the open window and head, unerringly and fatally, towards the bedside lamp she'd set carefully down on the floor so it gave enough light for her to read by but did not shine in Benji's eyes as he slept beside her. As she watched, trying ineffectually to shoo them away from the lethal lure, she felt a frightening sympathy with them. Rafaello di Viscenti was like that light—beautiful, irresistible, and quite deadly. She could so easily let herself be like one of the moths...

The rap came again, and, casting a nervous glance at Benji lest he wake, she scrambled off the bed and went to open the door.

Her jaw fell open.

Rafaello was standing there, looking breathtakingly attractive in charcoal trousers and a dark blue shirt whose open collar in no way made him look casual but instead gave him an air of Latin cool that made her breath catch helplessly in her throat.

'May I come in?' He stepped inside even as he spoke, his glance taking in the sleeping baby. 'Do I disturb you?'

Yes, screamed Magda inside her own head. You absolutely terrify me. You walk in here, looking like every woman's fantasy, and you ask if you disturb me.

Belatedly she summoned her scattered wits. 'No,' she gulped. 'Not at all.'

He nodded. The diffused light from the lamp on the floor turned his hair to sable and threw the planes of his face into edged relief. She felt her breath catch all over again.

'Dinner will be served shortly. Can you be ready in time?'

She stared gormlessly.

'One of the maids is coming to sit with the ch—' he caught himself, and amended his words. 'To sit with Benji. She will fetch you if he wakes.'

'He usually sleeps through until after midnight,' Magda said faintly, scarcely taking in what he had just said. 'Then he wakes, usually.' Except that last night, and the night before, Benji had slept soundly all night—exhausted, she fancied, after all the exertions and new experiences, as well as the silence of the Tuscan countryside. It had given her the first good sleep she'd had since he'd been born, and it had done her good, she knew. She was feeling far more rested than she usually did. Of course, she thought wryly, she was also living a life of total leisure at the moment. That helped as well…

'Good.' Rafaello was speaking again, and she forced herself to listen. 'Then I will leave you to change. Please be as quick as you can.'

His gaze flitted over her saggy T-shirt disparagingly.

She acknowledged him faintly and, nodding briefly, he took his leave.

Downstairs, he joined his aunt and uncle in the drawing room, to be greeted by the news from a poker-faced Giuseppe that his father had declared he was too ill to eat and retired to his bedroom. Rafaello's mouth tightened, but he said nothing about his father's obvious refusal to sit at the same table as his unwanted daughter-in-law.

His aunt was less forbearing.

'Impossible man!' exclaimed his aunt. 'I just hope this bride of yours has a thick skin, Rafaello.'

Her nephew's face shuttered. The familiar stab came again. A thick skin? She had needed that from the moment he had looked her over and decided she was the perfect vehicle of his revenge…

The sound of the door opening made him turn suddenly. As if his thoughts had summoned her, she was there, standing uncertainly in the doorway.

She looked like a mouse, he found himself thinking. She was wearing that atrocity of a frock, the same one she had married him in, with its hem hanging unevenly around her calves, no waist and a most unflattering sagging neckline, and her hair was tightly brushed back and knotted punishingly on the back of her head. The best that could be said about her was that she looked neat and clean-scrubbed.

'Good evening,' she said in a strangled voice that was scarcely audible.

For a moment the tableau held, and then, as he saw the colour—what there was of it—start to drain out of her face, Rafaello stepped forward and went up to her.

CHAPTER FIVE

'COME and meet my aunt and uncle.'

He took her elbow and drew her forward. She was as tense as a board under his touch, and she almost stumbled as she walked into the room until he let her go. Even then, as he stood by her side, he could see she was stiff as wood.

'Tia Elizavetta—this is Magda. Magda—my aunt, Elizavetta Calvi. And this is my uncle, *il professore* Bernardo Calvi.'

Magda felt her breath solidify in her lungs. Shock rippled through her. Rafaello di Viscenti had called her by her name.

Up till now it had been pointedly—painfully—obvious that he never addressed her by name, simply spoke directly to her. And this evening—her eyes widened in realisation—he had called Benji by his name as well! She could hardly believe it.

Nor could she believe that he was actually introducing her to his aunt and uncle. When she had walked in and seen them present she had steeled herself for another explosion like the one that had greeted her first presentation to Rafaello's family. But now, instead, the elegant woman in her discreetly stylish clothes who was his aunt was merely looking her over with gimlet eyes. She stood still, letting the woman inspect her. True, the woman's mouth had tightened as she perused her, but she hadn't gone apoplectic. Then, suddenly, the woman smiled at her. Not a huge smile, nor a very warm one, but a civil, social smile, and a smile for all that. She received a smile from the woman's husband as well, the professor, this time more warm if a little vague.

'Unfortunately,' Rafaello was saying in a remote voice, 'my father finds himself indisposed tonight. I hope you will excuse him.'

Magda bit her lip. It was perfectly obvious that Rafaello's father was avoiding her as if she had the plague. Well, she thought thinly, from his point of view I do. I'm hardly his ideal daughter-in-law. Oh, why on earth hadn't Rafaello realised that he should have chosen a woman from his own world if he'd wanted to avoid marrying his cousin? Instead he'd just rashly married the first woman he'd seen—she could recall that posh blonde's words with punishing clarity—and now look at the mess he was in. He should have thought a bit more about what his father's reaction was going to be to a wife who worked as a cleaner. *And* had a baby with her to boot. Didn't Rafaello care that that only made things worse?

Her chin lifted. Well, that was between Rafaello and his father. For herself, she couldn't care less if she earned her living cleaning the homes of rich people—or if Benji had no father. Benji was her life, Kaz's most precious gift to her—a final gift.

Giuseppe was clearing his throat and informing them that dinner was ready to be served. Rafaello moved closer to her and took her elbow once more. She tensed all over again. She knew it was nothing but show, but she wished he would stand about half a kilometre away from her. Then she forced herself to untense. She might as well be a block of wood as living flesh. She had not missed his disparaging look at her appearance, however swiftly it had been veiled.

Soon they were in the dining room, and Magda's eyes were shooting around the silk-hung room with its antique furniture. She was grateful to sit down at the gleamingly polished table.

Giuseppe and a pair of maids busied themselves serving the first course—delicate folds of Parma ham with sliced fresh pears, accompanied by a delicately flavoured white wine. Magda waited until the others had started eating, and then reached for whatever implements they had selected. As she took the first mouthful she paused, savouring the rich saltiness of the ham combined with the fresh nuttiness of the fruit.

'Is it to your taste?' Rafaello's aunt asked. Her English, though accented, was as impeccable as her nephew's.

'It's delicious.' Magda found herself answering spontaneously.

Signora Calvi smiled benignly. 'The pears are imported, alas, of which I do not approve—I, like most Italians, prefer to eat the fruits that are in season, and it is too early still for pears. But the ham is excellent. It is Parma ham—from a city perhaps better known in England for its cheese—parmesan.'

She was clearly going out of her way to make her feel comfortable, Magda realised. The kindness was appreciated, even if the explanation had been unnecessary. Parma ham was a familiar, if expensive item in British supermarkets these days, though doubtless quite inferior to what she was eating now.

'But there are many Tuscan specialities you will enjoy as well, I am sure,' Signora Calvi sailed on, placing an emphasis on Tuscan. 'Tuscany is famed for its simple cuisine, for dishes such as *bistecca alla fiorentina*, which is steak charred on coals, as well as duck and boar.'

Her husband held up a hand as he drank some of his wine. 'Do not be so harsh on poor Parma, my dear—after all, it shares a link with Tuscany, does it not?'

It was the first time Magda had heard Rafaello's uncle speak, apart from his quiet greeting to her, and he, like the rest of the family, spoke fluent English. His voice was a little dry, but good-humoured all the same. He glanced at her now, his face expectant, as though she were one of his students he was quizzing.

'This is Magda's first visit to Italy, Bernardo, she is unlikely to know your reference—' Rafaello's interjection was swift.

'The Duchess of Parma.' Magda spoke almost simultaneously as she remembered what her guidebook had told her. 'Marie-Louise, the Duchess of Parma and Napoleon's widow, was also the Duchess of Lucca.'

'Very good.' Professor Calvi beamed approvingly. 'You must be sure to visit Lucca very soon—it is a jewel of Tuscany.'

'I've read a little about it in the book I brought with me,' Magda replied. 'It is famous for its walls, I believe?'

'Yes, indeed. They were built at the end of the fifteenth century to repel the Spanish. Lucca succeeded in retaining its independence, and at one point was the only independent civic polity in Italy other than Venice—until Napoleon bestowed Lucca on his sister, Elisa, whom he also made Duchess of Tuscany.'

Magda frowned uncertainly. 'Was she the sister who was Queen of Naples?'

'No, that was Caroline, wife of his general, Murat. They, of course, replaced the deposed Bourbon monarchs of Naples, whose queen, also Caroline, has a rather romantic link with England.'

He paused again, clearly awaiting her answer. Magda cast about for the reference.

'She was friends with Lady Hamilton!' she remembered. 'That's where Emma Hamilton met Lord Nelson—in Naples.'

'Very good!' The approving beam came again.

'My husband is a historian, as you must already suspect,' his wife interjected dryly, having subjected Magda to a highly assessing and, she surmised, surprised look. 'Bernardo.' She turned to her husband. 'You must not be a bore.'

Magda smiled diffidently. 'History can never be boring—especially not in a country like Italy—there is just so much.'

She had said the right thing by the professor.

'And here in Tuscany is the richest history—even the name Tuscany hints at the earliest great Italian civilisation.'

'The Etruscans?' ventured Magda.

'The Etruscans,' confirmed the professor, and he was away, expansively expounding on the mysterious pre-Roman civilisation that had dominated the region long before Rome was mighty.

Magda was fascinated. All she knew came out of books, but here, across the table from her, was a native and an expert. She sat and listened, quite rapt, as Rafaello's uncle explained about the major Etruscan sites, their mysterious origins, strange religion and even stranger language that still remained undeciphered.

'I have always approved of the Etruscans,' put in his wife at one point. 'Their women were astonishingly liberated—they ate with the men and owned property, and were quite outspoken.'

Magda hid her smile. She could quite see why the formidable Signora Calvi should approve of such a state of affairs. She found she had glanced towards the head of the table, to see if Rafaello found his aunt's comment amusingly revealing, but when she looked at his face she stilled.

He was staring at her—simply staring at her—as if she'd sprouted extra arms and heads. She blinked, puzzled. Had she done something wrong? She looked away again, feeling her heart beating faster than it should. Was she behaving inappropriately? Was that it? Shouldn't she be putting herself forward and joining in the conversation, asking his uncle questions or presuming to answer them?

Then, across the table, she heard the professor say to Rafaello, 'Your wife will keep you busy for quite some time, my boy—you must take her on a tour. She has everything to see.'

She bit her lip again. The last thing Rafaello would want would be to be landed with taking her sightseeing.

'Oh, no,' she put in hurriedly, 'that would not be possible—my little boy...'

'I am sure your son will be quite content to be looked after by Maria and myself,' Signora Calvi replied calmly. 'This is ideal weather for touring.'

'Oh, no,' said Magda, disconcerted. 'Please—really— I couldn't leave Benji.'

'It will be good for him to develop the ability to be happy without your constant attendance,' pronounced Rafaello's aunt. 'You need have no anxiety about leaving him with us. Maria is extremely experienced with children, and she tells me he is a very good, well-brought up child, well advanced for his age. He is a credit to you, she tells me.'

She gave her benign smile, and Magda felt her colour rise. Her throat went tight. She stared down at her plate. Suddenly she felt a light touch on her hand.

'It has been hard for you, I think, no?' said Rafaello's aunt quietly. 'People will often make harsh judgements.'

She threw a deliberate look at Rafaello, who tightened his mouth. Then, with a deliberate change of subject, she said, 'Ring for Giuseppe, Rafaello. He may serve the next course.'

The remainder of the meal passed with relative ease. The professor, having discovered an eager listener in his nephew's bride, required very little prompting to continue his discourse, which ranged extensively over the history of Tuscany and that of Italy as a whole. Apart from a nagging worry over whether Benji was all right—even though she knew perfectly well that the smiling maid Gina was babysitting him—Magda found herself feeling less and less uncomfortable. It helped, too, that Rafaello said almost nothing, and that both his aunt and uncle seemed quite happy to let him remain as silent as he did.

It was not until Signora Calvi informed Giuseppe that

they would take coffee in the drawing room, and they got up from the table, that Rafaello was able to ask the question that had been infuriating him all evening.

As they stood back to let the professor and his wife leave the dining room, Magda felt her arm gripped.

'Perhaps you would like to tell me why,' demanded Rafaello, with a grim note in his voice that made her feel alarmed, 'given that you are quite evidently an educated woman, you earn your living in such a menial occupation.'

Magda stared up at him. He was too close to her again, but this time that was not the sole reason for her startled reaction.

'Educated?' she echoed.

'You have an excellent knowledge of history, for a start!' elucidated Rafaello bitingly. 'And you are obviously intelligent. So why do you work as a cleaner?'

Her face cleared. She was able to answer his question. 'I have no qualifications—I've always loved reading, but that's all. School was…difficult.' No need to bore him with the difficulty of being a child from a care home at a school where that was a cause for derision and mockery by more fortunate pupils. 'Although I did manage to get some GCSEs—they're the basic school leaving exams—I wasn't able to study any further.'

No need to tell him that that was the period when Kaz had first been diagnosed. 'But one of the things I would like to do, and you have made it possible—' she swallowed '—is to pursue further studies so that when Benji starts school I may be able to get some qualifications and get a better job eventually. I wouldn't work full time, of course, just during school hours. So I am always there for him.'

'Rafaello.' His aunt's voice came imperiously. 'Allow the poor child to have her coffee.'

Her arm was released and she was ushered with polite courtesy through to the drawing room.

'Come and sit beside me,' commanded Elizavetta Calvi,

having cast a shrewd look at her nephew and his wife, and she patted a space on the exquisite silk-upholstered sofa. 'Rafaello—Bernardo would like a cigar, but he is not to smoke in here. Be off with you both to the terrace, if you please.'

Subtlety clearly wasn't her strong point, thought Magda, and once again caught herself glancing at Rafaello. This time he met her eye, and for the barest second only amusement glimmered in them. And something else, too. A question. His aunt caught it, too.

'Magda will be perfectly safe,' she said caustically. 'She need tell me nothing she does not wish to.'

Personally, Magda had severe doubts about that, but the time she had spent over dinner had convinced her that, overbearing and autocratic as Elizavetta Calvi was, she was fundamentally well-meaning. There was no hostility directed at her.

And so it proved. Over two cups of coffee Rafaello's aunt proceeded to grill her comprehensively about her life, her job, her child and her reasons for marrying Rafaello di Viscenti. Only on one aspect did she hold back, to Magda's surprise—Benji's parentage.

'Such things happen,' she said bluntly. 'They always have and they always will. But I tell you, frankly I admire your courage in deciding to keep your child—it would have been so easy to have given him away.'

Never! The word leapt in Magda's throat, filling her with horror. More horror came on its heels—the knowledge that her own unknown birth mother had not even bothered to try and give her away. Simply left her to die in an alleyway. But she had survived, and with Benji would go on doing so.

Through the French windows she saw the silhouette of the man she had married for a hundred thousand pounds. Something kicked inside her, hard and painful. She looked away. No. That was pointless. Immature fantasy. Stupid and pathetic. He was not for her. Not even in her dreams.

She was awakened next morning by a maid bringing in a tray of coffee.

'*Buon giorno, signora,*' the girl said smilingly, cooing in Italian over Benji. He was still asleep, and Magda wondered at that as she sipped her fragrant coffee, looking out through the window to the tops of the cypress trees beyond, all bathed in morning sunlight.

She felt a wave of wellbeing go through her. All my life I'll remember this, she thought—how beautiful this place is. She felt sadness pricking at her that her time here was to be so short, before telling herself sternly that she was fortunate beyond belief to be here at all.

Her mind went back to the evening before, filling her with strange emotions. Rafaello's aunt and uncle had been so nice to her—and Rafaello had been so polite and civil, too! Signora Calvi hadn't even seemed to mind that she had married her nephew for money.

'Of course it is wrong,' she had said, in that unarguable fashion of hers, 'but it is quite understandable. I do not blame *you*, child.'

Magda frowned. Did that mean she blamed her nephew?

Heaviness filled her. Although she had walked into this minefield unwittingly, it was a still a horrible position to be in—everyone wishing you were a million miles away…

Benji's waking was a welcome diversion. He always woke in a playful, affectionate mood which could melt her even on days when she was half-dead with tiredness, let alone now, when her days were easy and her nights undisturbed.

Later, with both of them dressed, she picked up the coffee tray carefully with one hand, took Benji's small fingers with the other and set off for the kitchen and breakfast. But as she closed the bedroom door behind her she heard foot-steps coming along from the far end of the wide landing.

Rafaello's father was walking towards her. When he saw her, he stopped dead. Magda froze. Although she'd seen him only briefly that hideous afternoon three days ago, she knew it was Enrico di Viscenti immediately. He was far too much like Rafaello some thirty-odd years on.

His face hardened. Magda didn't know what to do. Say good morning? Say nothing? Go back into her bedroom?

Benji, sensing the atmosphere, wrapped his arms around her leg as she stood there, coffee tray in her hand, not having a clue what to do.

'So,' said Enrico di Viscenti in a harsh voice, 'you are still here.'

Magda said nothing. She didn't know what to say.

'Do you imagine you will make yourself a home here?' Enrico threw at her in that same harsh voice. 'Do you imagine yourself as a great lady now—you and your *bastardo*?'

She tensed all the way through her body.

Rafaello's father took a menacing step towards her. His dark eyes bored into hers, filled with fury and disgust.

'Then know this! My benighted son chose you to insult me. He threw it in my face that he defied my wishes so much he deliberately brought home a bride who is the low-est of the low. He chose you because you are the worst wife he could find—plain, ignorant, common, amoral. From the slums of London, cleaning toilets for a living. He chose you to disgust me.'

She thought she would faint. She could hear the blood drumming in her ears. Around her leg, Benji buried his face in the worn material of her cotton trousers and whimpered. He could not understand the words—but he could under-stand the anger, the raw hatred that came through. The con-tempt.

Her vision blurred. Rafaello's father strode past her, and she heard him descend the marble stairs to the hall below.

She felt the tray shaking in her hands and knew that if she did not put it down it would fall from her nerveless fingers and crash to the ground. But she couldn't stop her hands shaking.

Then, suddenly, the tray was taken from her.

'In here—'

She felt herself propelled back through the bedroom door—open again somehow—felt Benji lifted away, heard his protest, and then she was sitting on the bed, Benji in her arms. She just sat there clutching him, *clutching* him, not seeing anything, not feeling anything, just hunched there, holding Benji, who was whimpering in her arms.

Someone was standing in front of her. Tall and dark, blocking out the light. She knew who it was. Rafaello di Viscenti. Who had chosen her for his bride not because she was convenient and malleable but because she would disgust his father. She was the 'lowest of the low'—his father's hideous words rang like blows in her head—the perfect insult to throw in his father's face.

'Magda...'

His voice came low.

She went on clutching Benji to her and staring blindly down at the carpet, trying not to think, not to feel...

'You must not—must not believe what my father said. It is me he is angry with.' The words grated from him.

Her hand curved round Benji's head, his hair satin-smooth. She could say nothing. Nothing at all.

Rafaello watched the gesture. He wanted to find the words but he couldn't. There were none to find. His father had said them all. But he had to try, all the same.

'Magda, I—'

Her head lifted and her eyes met his. Hers were quite, quite blank.

'You don't have to say anything. It's quite unnecessary.' If her voice had a crack in it, she ignored it. Refused to acknowledge it. She would not feel anything; she *would* not. She stood up, settling Benji on to her hip. Another half-cracked breath seared from her. 'Please tell me where I should go for breakfast this morning—or would you prefer that I stayed here in my room?' Her voice was controlled, but it was thin—thin like wire pulled so taut it must surely break any instant.

Rafaello's mouth thinned.

'In summer the family has breakfast on the terrace. Come—'

He held out his hand to her. She ignored it, and walked to the door instead. Rafaello was there before her, opening it and letting her go through with a courtesy he would have afforded a duchess. Instead, she thought, with the peculiar blankness that seemed to have closed down over her, he's wasting it on *me*.

He chose you for that very reason, deliberately and calculatedly, to knowingly insult his father by his choice of bride. He'd known exactly how his father would react all along—he hadn't been thoughtless at all. He'd been cold-bloodedly set on using her to insult his father.

Family breakfast on the terrace was the very last thing that she wanted to endure, but the blankness would make it bearable after all. When she walked out with Rafaello she saw that his aunt and uncle were already there, as was his father.

Seeing Magda, the professor got to his feet and bade her good morning. She barely managed a nod in reply. With a scrape of iron on stone, Rafaello's father got to his feet, too. He picked up his full cup of coffee.

'I shall be in the library. I have matters to attend to.'

He walked away, making it obvious he refused to share her company.

The lowest of the low.

The words hit her again, and again.

Magda sat down, not where Rafaello was holding a chair for her, but at the farthest end of the table. She wanted to die, to sink through the floor. Her heart was in a vice, crushed with a pain she would not acknowledge.

'So,' said Elizavetta Calvi, her voice a little too loud, a little too determined, 'this is your little boy. And you said his name is—?'

'Benji,' said Rafaello, sitting down opposite Magda and flicking open his napkin. His voice was strained and Magda wondered why. Maybe it was the effort of giving her fatherless child his name.

She busied herself settling Benji on her lap, not meeting anyone's eyes, and one of the maids came out, bringing some warmed milk in Benji's feeding mug, which he gripped with delight and proceeded to imbibe gustily. For herself, she had no appetite. She seemed to be very far away, sitting behind a sort of glass wall that separated her from the others at the table, even when they spoke to her and she made brief, low-voiced, withdrawn replies. There was none of the drawing out or stimulating conversation of the night before.

'You are tired,' observed Rafaello's aunt, in a manner that was more a statement than a question.

Magda nodded in docile agreement, not meeting her eyes, feeding Benji a soft roll. Everyone was still very far away—especially Rafaello. He seemed to be light years away from her.

But he was watching her, she could see. His face was unreadable, and there was something shuttered about his eyes. Presumably, she thought, with that same remote, distant feeling that seemed to be pervading her whole brain, he is thinking how low and common I look, polluting his ancestral home. Wishing he could just dump me out with the trash.

Why did it hurt so much that Rafaello di Viscenti, a complete stranger to her in every meaningful definition of the word, should have deliberately and calculatedly used her to insult his father? Why did it hurt so much that he *wanted* her to be the lowest of the low, that he *wanted* to throw her in his father's teeth precisely because she was plain and common, a feckless single mother from the slums of London who cleaned toilets for a living?

She knew, with her head, that none of his litany of accusations was her fault, that she had nothing, *nothing* to be ashamed of. Someone had to clean toilets—and everything else. Someone had to keep the rich and pampered clean and comfortable. Those who did it were not shameful. To look down on someone because they were poor—*that* was shameful.

But she could tell herself that all she liked—somewhere, deep inside it just hurt that Rafaello di Viscenti had looked her over and catalogued every fact and factor about her that might disgrace his rich, well-bred, cultured, respectable family…and relished finding them so he could throw them in his father's face.

A scraping of chairs roused her from her painful reverie. Signora Calvi was speaking to her—Magda forced herself to listen.

'My dear, let Benji come with me for a while. Maria tells me one of her great-nieces has brought along some playthings her own children have outgrown. I believe there is a tricycle, and some toys that I am sure your little boy will adore. No, do not disturb yourself—he will come with me very happily, I have no doubt.'

She lifted Benji off Magda's lap and stood him on the terrace.

'*Vene.*' She smiled down at the infant. 'Come and see some new toys.'

'Toys' was a word Benji was pretty clued up on, and he toddled off happily, Signora Calvi holding one tiny hand, her husband the other. Magda watched the little procession make its way along the terrace and disappear around the corner of the house. She still felt dull, and numbed, and very far away inside.

Rafaello watched her watching them. She seemed very small, very young sitting there, far too young to have responsibility for a child.

Far too young to have to bear the cruel accusations his father had thrown at her.

His hands clenched on his thighs. *Dio*, she was hurt; it was obvious. There was a bleak, wounded look in her eyes which made him feel terrible. She'd withdrawn inside herself, shut herself away—and he couldn't blame her for that.

The feeling of discomfort he'd come to be familiar with around her sharpened acutely. Sharpened into guilt. He found himself wishing, with all his might, that he could undo the ugly scene that had played out in front of her bedroom door, that he could have stopped his father throwing those harsh, unpalatable insults in her face.

But Rafaello blamed himself, too. He had deliberately presented her to his father that first afternoon with a furious, sarcastic flourish, delineating every single unappealing, unflattering, unsavoury aspect of the woman he'd just married in order to ram home the message to his machinating father: You force my hand, force me to marry—well, look—look at the bride I've brought back with me.

Oh, he'd never intended the girl to find out—she wouldn't have understood what he'd shouted at his father—and yet, all the same, he had used her quite deliberately, used her wretched appearance and circumstances for his own ends.

Guilt flushed through him. A rare, unpleasant feeling.

And something more than guilt. Something that had started to spark in him all though that painful breakfast as he had sat there, watching her, watching her closed face, the wounded look in her eyes.

Anger.

An emotion very familiar to him over these last months as his father had sought to reel him in, tighter and tighter, into Lucia's grasping clutches. He'd lived with anger, day in, day out, until it had soaked all the way through him, obliterating everything else except his absolute, total determination not to let his father play with his life as if it were a toy. Yes, anger was a familiar feeling.

But this time there was something different about it. This time it was directed at himself.

With an abrupt movement he got to his feet.

'Come.'

Magda's eyes snapped away from where Benji and the Calvis had just disappeared. Rafaello was standing there, looking tall and commanding. Haltingly she stood up, dusting breadcrumbs from her trousers. As she looked up she saw Rafaello studying them disdainfully.

Yes, she thought silently, they are cheap, and unflattering, and hopelessly unfashionable. I do not wear them from choice, but necessity. If I had your money I would not wear them—but I don't, so I do. Poverty is not a crime. And it is not a cause for shame. I will not, she told herself, bow my head in disgrace for my lack of wealth. Nor will I bow it because I do not know who my parents were!

'Today,' announced Rafaello in a tight voice, 'we are driving to Lucca.'

Magda's eyes widened. She had not in the slightest expected this. Then she realised that it must be something to do with dinner last night, when the professor had talked about Lucca and his wife had urged her nephew to take his bride touring.

'It is quite unnecessary,' she said. Her voice was low and blank.

'You will,' replied Rafaello, 'allow me to be the judge of that.'

She sensed anger in him beneath the clipped words. She could not be surprised. His aunt had chivvied him, in her imperious fashion, to take her sightseeing, and it was obvious he would not be too thrilled at the prospect of not only wasting a good day but wasting it in the company of a woman he had chosen for being the lowest of the low...

'I can't leave Benji,' she said. She couldn't meet his eyes, she found. Hers were focussing somewhere just below, where the smooth strong column of his throat rose out of the open-necked top of his polo shirt. She found that was not a good place to focus and shifted her gaze a little lower. But that meant her gaze was now eyeballing the broad expanse of his pectoral muscles, straining at the knitted fabric of the polo shirt, descending to the narrow leanness of his abdomen.

She flicked her gaze so that it was staring harmlessly over his shoulder instead, at a distant cypress tree edging the gardens.

'Benji will be fine,' Rafaello said, with the dismissiveness of a childless man for the neurotic anxieties of a mother. 'Between Maria and my aunt he will do very well, be assured—they are both very taken with him.' He glanced at his watch—a thin, expensive-looking circlet of gold on his strong wrist. 'I should like to set off in half an hour. Please be ready.'

He nodded at her and was gone, striding off indoors.

She sighed. What should she do? Dig her heels in and refuse to go with him? She certainly wanted to. The very thought of having to spend any time at all with him was anathema, let alone being dutifully carted around sightseeing by a man who wished her to perdition. What on earth was he doing this for? Surely he could have come up with some excuse about pressing matters of work to distract his aunt from her evident determination to pack them off together? And it didn't matter what he said—she did not like to leave Benji. She'd never spent any time away from him at all—ever.

Yet when she went off in search of him she found that he was not missing her at all. Maria and Rafaello's aunt were making a huge fuss of him, and he had an exciting push-along trike to ride. The housekeeper hurried over to her.

'Go,' she instructed her. 'The little one will be very happy. He does not notice you are not here. If he sees you he will want you. So go now. Yes, yes, if he is unhappy without you I shall phone Signor Rafaello on his mobile phone, and he will return you at once. He has promised me. But we shall take care of the boy as if he were ours. And I have cared for many, many children—go, go now.' She shooed Magda away and returned eagerly to Benji, volubly admiring his prowess on his vehicle.

Reluctantly she turned and left. She knew that it was sensible for Benji to start being happy away from her, for when she returned to England and bought a proper place of her own to live it would be time to start introducing Benji to playgroups and nursery school.

But it still pulled at her terribly as she went up to her room to tidy herself and change into something very slightly less shabby. She had a cotton skirt with her, khaki-coloured, which although it hung on her hips was at least a skirt. She put on a white cotton short-sleeved blouse with it, slipped an olive-green jumper into her capacious bag that seemed strangely empty without its usual complement of baby stuff, and then went downstairs again. She ached to go and check on Benji again, but knew it would be counter-productive.

She stood in the hall, wondering what to do, hoping that whatever happened she would not meet Rafaello's father. But with any luck he was in that room with closed double doors—she could hear opera wafting out of it. Verdi, by the sound of things. Though she owned no hi-fi, she had scraped enough money to buy a small portable cassette player and radio, and usually spent the evenings once Benji was asleep reading and listening to the wealth of current affairs, arts and science programmes available, as well as her favourite classical music stations.

Rapid footsteps on the stairs made her turn. Rafaello was descending—looking, she thought as her breath caught in her lungs, like some Roman god coming down to earth, all lithe power and grace in dark, immaculately cut chinos and his pale, open-necked polo shirt. A silk-lined jacket was hooked over his shoulder with his finger, and from the other hand dangled a pair of sunglasses. She stood, battered bag held in front of her with both hands, awaiting his bidding and trying to stop thinking that he was the most beautiful male object in the universe.

'You are ready? Good.' His tone was brisk, impersonal, the way it usually was when he was required to address her.

He headed for the front door, and reluctantly she went after him. Outside, the sun dazzled her, and she blinked, following his crunching footsteps over the gravel as he headed around to the back of the villa.

'Wait,' he instructed her, as they arrived at what was evidently a row of garages. Dutifully she did so, and he headed inside one of them. A moment later a loud, throaty roar sounded—like a dragon disturbed in its lair. A monstrous beast of an open-topped car emerged slowly, gleaming scarlet and bearing the easily recognisable insignia that marked it as a top-of-the-range sports car.

Rafaello nosed it round to position it beside Magda. Then he leaned across and opened the door.

'Get in—'

She did, very trepidatiously, and seemed to sink almost right down to the ground. Just as she was getting her bearings he leant across her, reaching for the seat belt.

She froze. He'd never been this physically close to her, and it was unnerving. She shrank back into the deep bucket leather seat, and tried not to feel that at any moment her breasts would brush his arm. Then, just as swiftly, he was gone again, sitting back in the driver's seat. He slipped his dark glasses over his eyes, put the car into gear, and roared off.

Magda hung on for dear life, as if she were on a roller-coaster, as they headed down towards the autostrada running along the valley of the River Arno.

She stared ahead, and around, as the Tuscan landscape shot by her, blurred by speed, and glanced at Rafaello's hands on the steering wheel. They curved around it, tensile and expert, tilting and twisting just enough to manoeuvre the awesomely powerful car just the way he wanted it, dropping one hand repeatedly to the gearstick to change gears relentlessly up and down as the journey required.

He seemed, Magda thought, to be working something out of his system.

CHAPTER SIX

THE walls of Lucca were as spectacular as her guidebook had promised, girdling the ancient city and topped with plane trees to make, she could see, an elevated walkway.

But the walls were not Rafaello's destination, nor the medieval cathedral of San Martino, nor any of the city's host of churches within the ancient *centro storico*, nor the art museum, nor the Puccini museum which commemorated one of Lucca's most famous sons. Instead, Magda found herself being walked up to a narrow building with an elegant frontage, in one of the lanes that led off the fashionable Via Fillungo. She had been going along in a daze, her neck craning crazily as she took in all around her. Wherever she looked were the wonders of an ancient Tuscan city, drenched in history: the *palazzos* and the churches, the cafés and the restaurants, and she soaked up the architectural glory that was Italy.

'Come,' said Rafaello, and ushered her inside the doorway.

A brightly lit reception desk faced her, staffed by a chicly-dressed woman in her twenties. She looked up from an appointments book as they entered, and her face lit up.

'Rafaello.' She launched into voluble Italian, coming around from behind her desk and lavishing kisses on both his cheeks, openly hugging him. He said something to her with a laugh, clearly at ease with her. Then he began to talk.

Magda stood uncomfortably a little way away, aware from the expression on the woman's face, and the little glances she threw at her from time to time as she heard Rafaello out, interjecting a few questions of her own, that she was the object of their conversation. She clutched her bag awkwardly and felt the colour rising dully in her cheeks. She was just about to turn away and stare out through the window on to the narrow street outside when the woman gave a delighted laugh, clapped her hands, and turned to Magda.

'Come, come,' she said brightly in English, 'there is *so* much to do, and so little time. But, oh, the result will be *favoloso!*'

She beckoned to her smilingly. 'Rafaello we send away—he is quite useless here, and I have no wish for his opinions.' She glanced at him humorously. *'Vattene! Vattene! A piu tardi.'* She made shooing gestures with her hands.

Magda finally found her voice. 'Please—what is happening?'

The woman's dark eyes sparkled mischievously. 'A surprise!'

Magda looked anxiously at Rafaello, hands clenching each other over the worn strap of her bag. His face was unreadable, but abruptly he said something to the woman, who, giving an understanding nod, headed out through a door at the rear of the room. He looked at Magda a moment as she stood there, visibly anxious.

'There is nothing to worry about,' he said. His voice came more tersely than he had intended. 'Just place yourself in Olivia's hands and you will be fine.'

'I don't understand,' she said stiffly.

He looked down at her a moment longer. Then, as if finding the words difficult, he said, 'If I could undo what you heard my father say this morning I would do so. But I cannot. All I can do,' he finished, 'is disprove it.'

Her face stilled. It was like a mask sliding over her face—the way it had been when he had taken her back into her room, the way it had been at breakfast. Giving her a wall to hide behind—a wall to shield her from what she had heard his father tell her.

Only the eyes gave her away. He could see the hurt in them.

'But you can't disprove it,' she said quietly, her voice quite expressionless. 'Because it is the truth, isn't it? What your father said? I was…am…the perfect insult to throw at him. The total opposite of anything your family could possibly welcome as a bride. And that's why you married me. That's exactly why you married me and not someone from your own world. To insult your father.'

He made a noise in his throat as though he was going to speak, but she went on. 'I told you it didn't matter, and it doesn't. You are paying me a hundred thousand pounds, and for that I have no business to make a fuss.'

She spoke quite steadily, but all the same there was something not quite right with her voice.

Something twisted inside Rafaello like a knife in his gut. 'You say it is the truth, Magda—but it isn't. You've already proved it a lie to me—and to my aunt and uncle, and Maria and Giuseppe. Now I just want to finish the job.'

She stared at him. 'What part is a lie? Tell me? That Benji has no father? That I dress like something left on a rubbish dump? That I clean toilets for a living? That I am so far from being the sort of female who could be your wife that I might as well be a clod of earth underfoot? What part is a lie?'

A nerve started to tick in his cheek. She was looking at him quite expressionlessly, but he felt emotions surging inside him. One was anger, that same brand of anger that had driven him this morning. But there was more than anger.

Guilt. It burned him like acid.

He spelt out his repudiation to her. 'You are not the first woman to have a child outside marriage. It is no longer the stigma it once was—even here in Italy. And we have already discussed your situation—you obviously have the intelligence to be something far more, and one day, when you are freed from the drudgery of poverty, you shall be. Your origins are not your fault, any more than your son's are his. And as for your appearance—well, that is about to be dealt with.'

He turned his face away from her—he did not want to see her looking at him, hiding the hurt behind that shuttered mask she had put over her face. 'Olivia.' He spoke in Italian and the woman emerged, an enquiring look on her face.

'It is all explained?' she said in English. 'Good.' She smiled at Magda again. 'Now we begin.'

'I will return later,' said Rafaello to Magda, and walked out.

She stared after him helplessly. What should she do? Should she go after him and tell him…? Tell him what? Tell him she'd like to do something else—like go back to London and never lay eyes on him or his family or his precious Tuscan villa ever again? Well, she couldn't. She had signed papers—a contract, a wedding certificate—and there was nothing whatsoever she could do until Rafaello di Visenti decided it was time to send her back to England without risking any possibility of the marriage being declared fraudulent and invalid and so play right into his father's hands again.

'Come this way,' said Olivia in her bright, smiling voice. With a dull, numb feeling of resignation, Magda followed her.

Rafaello sat at the café looking out over the piazza which had once been a Roman amphitheatre, two thousand years ago. Apart from making one single purchase, he'd cooled his heels for well over two hours now, spending the time moodily striding around the city, wandering in and out of the countless churches, ignoring, as he always did when he

wasn't in a receptive mood, the more than frequent glances
he received from tourist and Italian females alike.

It had been impulse—impulse and guilt—that had made
him yank that poor scrawny creature out of the villa this
morning and throw her into Olivia's clutches to improve
upon nature somehow—anyhow. But maybe he had not
done the girl any favours by letting Olivia loose on her. He
frowned. Maybe the material Olivia had to work on was
hopeless! Maybe he had only set her up for yet another
round of humiliation at his hands...

Hadn't he already humiliated her enough?

He gestured for another cup of coffee and picked up his
newspaper again. Perhaps the miseries of the world at large
would take his mind off his guilt.

Some forty minutes later his mobile sounded. Reaching
inside his jacket pocket, he flicked it on.

'Pronto—'

'Rafaello?' It was Olivia. 'We're all done. We'll meet
you at the restaurant. See you there.'

He made his way to the restaurant where he'd reserved
a table for lunch. Inside, he spotted Olivia immediately, by
the crowded bar area. She saw him and gave a wave. He
headed towards her, wondering what she'd done with
Magda. Misgiving filled him again—perhaps Olivia had
found it so impossible to make the girl presentable and had
left her behind in the salon while she conveyed the bad
tidings to him.

As he approached, a woman seated with her back to him
at the bar caught his eye. There were a good many females
in the place, but this one definitely caught his attention. His
eyes flickered over her. She was sitting very straight, and
very still. She was wearing a sleeveless shift in dark cin-
namon raw silk. She was very slender, with a long, elegant
back. Her hair, a delicate, unusual shade of light brown,
skilfully coloured, he realised, with soft amber highlights,
rested in a sleek wave over her shoulders, lightly flicked at

the ends. Interesting, he found himself thinking. Something different. Intriguing. He wanted her to turn, so he could see if she looked as good from the front as the back.

Then, remembering this was hardly the occasion to be assessing the charms of other women, he dragged his eyes back to Olivia. She was watching him approach, his gaze clearly taken by the woman at the bar. He reached her and greeted her with the customary kiss on either cheek.

'Well—how did it go?' he asked in Italian. Mentally he prepared himself for the worst. He glanced around, but there was still no sign of Magda.

'See for yourself,' replied Olivia in a curious voice. If he hadn't known better he'd have said that she was trying not to burst out laughing. He glanced around, still not seeing the poor dab of a girl he'd thrust at Olivia that morning. Resolutely he ignored the intriguing woman with her back to him—he must not eye her up. She would just have to be one that got away, that was all.

'Magda—' said Olivia, and Rafaello saw her lips twitching as she watched him *not* looking at the woman seated at the bar. Clearly it amused her that he wanted to study another woman when his only concern should be what Olivia had managed to do with the one he'd handed over to her more than three hours ago.

Even so, as he glanced around for Magda, he couldn't help noticing from the corner of his eye that the woman at the bar had chosen that very moment to swivel slowly on her seat. He couldn't resist it. He turned to look at her.

For a moment he just stared, disbelieving. There was something wrong with his eyes—there had to be. The woman at the bar had Magda's face.

But it wasn't Magda's face—it was the face of a stunning female that was drawing more eyes than his.

'*Dio mio,*' he breathed. '*Non posso crederici!*'

Olivia gave a crow of delight, but Rafaello ignored her. He was still staring, still disbelieving. It was Magda, but it wasn't Magda. Her unprepossessing features had all been subtly rearranged, it seemed, and the effect was extraordinary. It wasn't just the make-up that Olivia had applied—skilful though that was—it was more. Her skin was not sallow and blemished, it was flawless. There was no pale pastiness but a beautiful, translucent glow about her. Her eyes were deeper, larger—quite beautiful. Her narrow face was delicate, framed by that fall of gleaming, polished hair, her cheekbones were sculpted, drawing attention to those beautiful eyes. And her mouth...

He felt a kick in his stomach. Her mouth simply made him want to slide his hand beneath that fall of hair and bring his own mouth down...

'You like?'

It was Olivia's deliberately arch, openly teasing voice that brought him back. But only momentarily. His eyes slid back to the woman he hardly recognised, moving from her face to drink in the rest of her. She was as slender from the front as the back—not scrawny. *Dio*, how could he have thought her scrawny? She was like a willow, pliant and graceful. The simple, superbly cut line of her shift delineated each breast, not full, but high and softly rounded...

He could not take his eyes off her.

And she was staring back at him. Staring with that same expression of stunned disbelief as his. He wondered why. Then he stopped wondering and went back to working his eyes down her slender body, right down her gazelle-like legs and then back up to her face again.

Absently he felt a slight kiss brush against his cheek, heard a soft, '*Ciao*, Rafaello—enjoy...' as Olivia slipped past him, but he paid no attention.

'Magda?' His voice husked, as if it were not working quite properly.

She bit her lip, and with that familiar gesture he suddenly accepted that this really, truly was the poor dab of a creature he'd so arrogantly made use of for his own self-obsessed ends and treated with total indifference as a god-sent tool, ideal for his single purpose—to confound his father.

Emotions warred within him. Some familiar, some completely new. Up to now, the best emotion he'd been able to come up with for her had been pity—a sort of careless, almost contemptuous pity for so unlovely and wretched a member of her sex. Pity shot with guilt that he'd exposed her to the vituperation of his father, his lashing out at her, forcing a knowledge upon her that had been vicious in its cruelty.

He had never meant her to realise why he had chosen her. Never meant her to have that cruel truth thrown at her.

The twist in his guts came again.

You thought that you could just pay her, and she'd put up and shut up.

Well, he knew better now. His father had held a mirror up to him, and the sight had not been pleasant. Hearing his own litany of condemnation echoed by his father had made him realise, horribly, for the first time, just how callous he had been.

But he intended to make it up to her. To prove his father wrong. To prove himself wrong!

And, *Dio*, how he was being proved wrong!

The emotions battled inside him. The guilt was becoming familiar now, but the second was completely new—and blew him away.

It was desire.

Magda was reeling. Reeling and whirling in a kind of white-out blur of emotions which were swirling inside her head so tempestuously she could scarce make sense of them. She caught at one, the easiest one to catch, and knew that it was shock, sheer shock and disbelief, that Rafaello di Viscenti—beautiful, arrogant, breathtakingly gorgeous Rafaello di Viscenti, who was as far removed from her as if he were one of the gods of old—was looking her over as if she were…as if she were a woman—a real, flesh-and-blood female with face and hair and breasts and limbs—all the accoutrements of a woman. A woman worthy of looking over.

It was as if she'd just snapped into existence for him. As if before, as she had known with a shame that only a plain, undesirable female could know, she had simply not existed as a female to him at all. All she had been to him was something it would not occur to him to look at, and when he had he'd left her feeling that she was covered in slime. Repulsive to him.

But now—now it was as if someone had truly sprinkled fairy dust over her and brought her to radiant life in his eyes. She was there, in front of him—a living, breathing woman. And he was looking her over. Very, very thoroughly.

And that lit the fuse for the second emotion that was sending her reeling. The impact of being inspected, head to toe, by Rafaello di Viscenti, as a fully paid-up member of the female sex worthy of his attention was just devastating—like being caught in a beam of high-power light that licked like flame all over her.

The moment seemed to go on for ever and ever, and then dimly Magda became aware that someone was standing beside them, deferentially proffering two large leather-bound menus. The man murmured something and Rafaello dragged his eyes from Magda and took the menus, replying distractedly.

'What would you like to eat?'

There still seemed to be a husk in his voice that Magda had never heard before, and it served to send a little tingle up her spine. But then her whole body was tingling.

And not just because she'd been caught in Rafaello di Viscenti's devastating eyeline. The three hours she'd spent in Olivia's clutches had been the most extraordinarily ter-

rifying and exhilarating experience. She had simply yielded
to the other woman's smiling enthusiasm and let herself be
stripped naked, hair unpinned, inspected, tut-tutted over,
before being worked on in a major, major way.

Magda hadn't known such beauty treatments existed!
She'd been wrapped up in weird stuff, neck to toe, had her
face slathered and unslathered; her body had been rubbed
and polished and waxed and smoothed and creamed. Her
hair had been washed and conditioned and coloured and
cut and blown and styled. And then Olivia had approached
with a treasure chest of make-up and proceeded to paint a
face on her that she simply had not believed when she saw
it reflected in the mirrors of the changing room where
Olivia had selected from a range of beautiful clothes. She
had stared, dumbstruck, as Olivia had slipped a cool, silky
shift over her head, zipped it swiftly up the back and stood
away.

'What did I tell you?' Olivia had said softly. 'That I
would make you look *favoloso*. And I have.'

She had, too, and Magda was still walking on air, feeling
like Cinderella must have felt when the fairy godmother
had finished with her. She had stammered her thanks in-
coherently to the other woman, who had laughed, and said,
'Good—now we show you off to Rafaello and watch his
jaw fall to the floor.'

And so it would have—if Rafaello di Viscenti had been
capable of so inelegant a reaction. As it was, just seeing
that look of stupefaction mingled with that tingle-inducing,
shiver-making, blush-urging looking over had swept away
all Magda's fears and misgivings that perhaps Olivia had
got it totally, totally wrong…

She tensed. Rafaello was leaning towards her, his shoulder almost touching hers as he reached out a hand to run
down her menu.

'Would you like me to translate?' he asked.

She wasn't capable of reciting the alphabet at this moment in time, let alone working out a menu written in Italian.

She swallowed. 'I...I'll just have something simple, please,' she managed to get out in a whispery sort of voice.

His glance flicked to hers and she suddenly saw the golden lights in his dark eyes, swept by those long, impossible lashes, caught the heady scent of his oh-so-masculine aftershave...and his own, even more masculine scent.

She felt faint, breathless.

He drew back. 'Very well.' He gave a smile, and the way his mouth indented, altering the planes of his face, made her feel faint again. She had seen him smile before— at his aunt last night, at Olivia this morning—but this time...this time the smile was for her. Faintness drummed at her again. This couldn't be happening. It was like a dream...

But if it was a dream, it was one that she didn't wake up from. Rafaello took her elbow, his hand burning on her skin, doing extraordinary things to her insides, which had a whole flock of butterflies soaring away invisibly, and led her through the restaurant out into a tiny cobbled courtyard at the back, decked with flowers and set with shaded tables.

She took her place, terrified she was going to stumble on her unaccustomed high heels, but there was no mishap, and she was sitting there, beneath the awning, with eyes for no one and nothing except Rafaello di Viscenti.

For a while, as he got on with the business of ordering food and wine, she was left in peace simply to drink him in, to tell herself that it could only be a dream, that she was not really sitting here, transformed by a magic wand, with the most beautiful man in the world. Then, ordering done, Rafaello turned back to her.

There was something in his eyes that made all the butterflies swoop upwards in one soaring flight.

'It is *incredibile*!' he said to her, and his eyes flickered over her face, her hair, her torso. 'I do not know what to say.' He spread his hands in a very Italian gesture.

Magda shifted uncomfortably. 'It's the make-up and everything.' Her voice was strained.

'Everything?' Rafaello echoed. 'Yes, everything. I have been blind—quite blind.' There was something curious about his voice, and her eyes met his. There was a strange expression in them that made her feel...feel what?

She could not put a name to it.

He was talking again.

'Blind to everything,' he said. 'And now I ask you...' his voice changed '...if you will forgive my blindness and accept a peace offering.' He slipped a hand inside his jacket pocket.

He extracted a little flat, circular packet, exquisitely wrapped in silvery tissue with a golden ribbon, the fruit of his shopping that morning, and placed it in front of her.

'Open it,' he said, in that same curious voice.

Uncertainly, but obediently, she did so. As the ribbon fell away so did the tissue, revealing, unmistakably, a blue velvet jewel case. With the butterflies jostling in her stomach, she lifted the lid.

Inside was a necklace, fine and delicate, made of intricately woven gold in a design that was as skilful as it was beautiful. She stared at it, blinking.

'Will you accept it as a token of my regret for my treatment of you?'

His voice was low, and there was still that note in it she could not identify. But she was in no state to analyse his tone of voice.

Her throat tightened. 'I can't take this,' she got out. 'Please—it is quite unnecessary. You are paying me so much money that—'

Her words were cut off. Rafaello's hand had snaked out and set down on hers.

'No,' he said, and there was a sharpness in his voice that

made her look at him almost fearfully. 'Of that we will not speak. Now…' his voice changed again '…if you like the necklace put it on. It will go well, I think, with what you are wearing.'

Yes, thought Magda desperately, that's how I must think of it—as nothing more than an accessory to the dress. And the dress, and everything else that Olivia did to me, is just part of what Rafaello wants. He's got fed up with having such an eyesore in his house, and he's done something about it. Don't, *don't* read anything more into it. You mustn't, you *mustn't*!

So, obediently, she picked up the necklace, which was light as a feather in her fingers, and made to put it on. Her fingers fumbled at the back of her neck, trying to fasten it. In a moment Rafaello was there, his hands sliding away her fall of hair and his fingers brushing hers as he took the necklace from her.

'Allow me…' he murmured, and started to fasten the necklace.

The butterflies inside her went crazy—and every drop of blood in her body dropped to her feet. She gasped as the nerve-endings in the delicate nape of her neck quivered with exquisite sensation.

If she could capture that moment for ever she would glimpse heaven, she thought, her eyes fluttering shut as she gave herself to the lightest, most blissful feeling.

Then it was gone, and so was Rafaello, back in his seat, viewing his handiwork.

And her.

'Today,' he said softly, and his eyes drank her in like a rare, vintage wine, 'we start again.'

The whole day was like a dream—and Rafaello was like a different person, Magda thought. As if he had never looked at her and seen nothing more than the last person his father would welcome as his son's bride. That Rafaello seemed to have vanished. Now there was only a man—the most beautiful man in the world to her—sitting opposite her and treating her as if she were a princess. It was a heady, heady feeling, and she had to try very hard to keep her feet on the ground, lest she soar upwards with the butterflies that stayed with her all through lunch, fluttering inside.

Over lunch, which seemed to last for ever and yet but a moment, he kept the conversation very impersonal. He told her about Lucca, and Tuscany, and Italy, and conversation ranged from the historical to the contemporary, as he regaled her with the mores and the customs of modern Italians.

Even though she felt awkward at first, and could only respond to his conversation in stilted phrases, gradually, as the wine in her glass went down, she slipped into the kind of enquiring questioning she'd given his uncle the evening before, and found herself relaxing and talking normally. She drank it all in, storing the time away as a precious memory, a dream that seemed, quite unbelievably, to be happening in real life. And all the time, as they talked, she was aware of a current running like electricity through her body, making it harder and harder to refrain from doing what she just ached to do—stare and stare at the homage to male beauty that was the perfection of Rafaello di Viscenti.

It was as lunch ended that another reality finally penetrated.

Benji.

With a pang of guilt she said, as Rafaello placed his credit card on the table for the waiter to collect, 'Please— would it be possible—may I phone Maria—to see if Benji is all right?'

'Of course.' He smiled his ready assent.

He extracted his mobile, dialled and spoke rapidly, then disconnected.

'Benji has had an excellent morning, eaten a hearty

lunch, and is now sleeping peacefully,' he reported. 'However, Maria suggests that it would be good if you were there when he wakes. In which case perhaps we shall leave a more extensive tour of the city for another occasion, and content ourselves with making nothing more than a short *passagiata* along a section of the walls. It is a very pleasant stroll to take.'

Under any circumstances the walk along the famous walls of Lucca would have been pleasant, but for Magda it was blissful. She worried a little that her feet would be pinched in the beautiful cinnamon-coloured high heels that Olivia had procured for her, but the leather was so soft, the fit so perfect, that there was no problem at all. Only, as she walked she was conscious of the effect of the high heels, how they lifted her hips and made her sway.

Self-consciously, as they moved out on to the bright sun-lit pavement from the restaurant, she fished inside the stylish handbag that matched the shoes and extracted the pair of dark glasses that Olivia had bestowed upon her. It was much easier, wearing sunglasses, to look without being seen. And as they strolled along, Rafaello's hand attentively at her elbow, she realised with a kind of disbelieving shock that they were drawing attention. At first she thought it was just that women were looking at Rafaello, a highly understandable phenomenon, but then she became aware that she, too, was drawing eyes.

Men were looking at her, quite openly, quite obviously, as they walked past, or they looked across at her from the cafés. It was so blatant that she felt as if she had no clothes on, and found she had pressed closer, quite unconsciously, to Rafaello.

He glanced down at her, a wry smile indenting his mouth.

'In Italy we are not shy about admiring a beautiful woman. Do not worry—with me beside you they will do no more than look. But—' his voice became dry 'I do not advise that you tour on your own—you would be like a honeypot to every man around.'

She felt herself colouring—and heard Rafaello's words humming in her head.

He called me a beautiful woman!

In a daze, she walked on.

Along the walls it was easier. There were more tourists here, and she felt she drew less attention. She moved a little away from Rafaello again, and he let her be, simply strolling beside her, constraining his pace to hers.

It was a leisurely progress as Rafaello stopped to point out landmarks on both the city side of the walls and the outer sides.

'The wealthy Lucchesi in the sixteenth century built their summer villas in the countryside around the city, and several are open to view. Perhaps we shall go and visit one another day. There is so much to see in Tuscany you will be spoilt for choice.'

'Please,' said Magda, awkward suddenly, 'you do not have to take me around. I am perfectly happy staying in the villa—I am sure you must be very busy with work and so on.'

'There is nothing that needs my urgent attention,' Rafaello said dismissively. The board meeting to confirm him as chairman would not take place until the following week. The delay did not alarm him—his father would not, *could* not, for his pride's sake, renege on the unholy bargain he had struck with his son.

His mind flicked away. He did not want to think about his father right now. Too much anger roiled beneath the surface. A grim smile flickered on his mouth. When they returned he would force his father to acknowledge Magda—wipe out the ugly, cruel litany he had thrown at him, that was choking in his father's craw.

He glanced down at the silky head that barely reached to his shoulders. He could still not get over the transformation. It was, indeed, incredible. She walked along beside him, high heels doing all sorts of miraculous things to her posture, and the dress, blessedly simple—though he knew the bill for anything that simple, that superbly cut, would be astronomical—doing the most amazing things to her figure. As for the rest of her—well, it was a dream. Not scrawny, but wand-slim. Not plain and pasty but…radiant. That was the only word for her now.

She would grace any setting—and he would make his father see that. Make him acknowledge her intelligence, her education—self-taught, and all the more credit to her, he thought soberly, given her grim financial circumstances. Make him see that every cruel description of her had been wrong—see even that it had been her devotion to her baby that had made her stoop to such menial work as he had found her in.

A frown flickered in his eyes.

Abruptly, without thinking, he spoke.

'Tell me about Benji's father.'

Magda halted in mid-step, then started walking again. There had been a harshness in Rafaello's voice that took her aback. Why did he want to know?

Slowly, she framed the words. 'It…it isn't easy to tell,' she answered. 'You see,' she went on, looking ahead of her, 'when I was in the home—'

'Home?'

'Children's home—care home. An orphanage—I don't know what it would be in Italian.'

'*Brefotrofio.*' He frowned. What was this? She had been an *orfano*? 'What happened to your parents?'

'I…I don't know.'

'*Come?*'

She risked a glance at him. He was frowning. It made him look intimidating.

'How is it you do not know?' he pursued.

'I…I don't know who my parents were. I…I was found,

when I was a few hours old. The police tried, without success, to trace the woman…well, girl, really, I suppose—most women who abandon their babies are very young; she was probably a teenager, pregnant by mistake and terrified, which is why…why she just wanted to get rid of me.' Her voice was strained. 'It's very understandable.'

Her voice trailed off. Rafaello said nothing. She went on walking. 'So, you see,' she continued in the same strained voice, though she tried very hard to make it as normal-sounding as possible, 'I don't know who my mother was, and I have no idea at all about my father—well, the boy who fathered me, presumably equally by mistake. Maybe he didn't even know he'd got my mother pregnant. Or maybe—' her voice tightened '—my mother didn't even know which boy had got her pregnant. So, anyway…' She took a breath. 'I was taken into care, and—'

Cold was running down Rafaello's spine. 'I knew nothing of this!'

His interruption made Magda flinch. The harshness was back in his voice with a vengeance. Her feet slewed to a halt. The fragile edifice of civility which had been built up over lunch crashed down around her ears. She stole a look at him. He had stopped, too, and stood looking down at her. His eyes, veiled behind his dark glasses, were invisible, but his mouth was set in a tight, grim line.

Her heart plunged to the ground. It was like walking headfirst into a blizzard after spring flowers had blossomed. Oh, why didn't I just make some excuse and tell him nothing about Benji—or me? she thought in anguish. He's horrified—appalled! She felt sick inside.

'I…I thought you knew,' she said in a small, shaky voice. 'It was on my birth certificate. "Parents unknown." And my time of birth was the closest estimate the hospital could come up with. You wanted my birth certificate for the marriage licence.'

'I did not see it,' he replied remotely.

Magda bit her lip. Of course. Why should Rafaello di Viscenti bother himself with trivia like her birth certificate?

'You were telling me about Benji's father.' The voice that prompted her was distant still. With a heavy, sinking heart, Magda forced herself to continue her sorry tale.

'Um—it was in the care home—there was another inmate. Kaz. We sort of…stuck together… Then—well, um—it gets…complicated.' She swallowed through her tightening throat, forcing out words that brought back so many agonising memories. 'We'd just left the home, let loose on the world, and we were living together when Kaz was diagnosed with cancer. At first the treatment worked, for a couple of years, but then the cancer came back. Terminal this time. Kaz…Kaz died just after Benji was born….'

She couldn't go on. Just couldn't. She started walking again, but she couldn't see anything. She was grateful for her dark glasses because they kept the tears hidden. Her steps were jerky.

Suddenly her arm was taken. Held in an iron grip. She tried to pull away, but she could not. She felt tears seeping from under the lower rim of the dark glasses, and lifted a hand to try and wipe them away.

'I am ashamed,' came the low voice. 'I am ashamed of everything I have ever thought or said about you.'

He turned her towards him, taking her other elbow in that vice-like grip. She screwed up her eyes, trying to stop the tears coming. Her throat was burning with the effort of keeping herself from crying.

She felt one hand let her go, and then he was sliding her dark glasses from her eyes.

'No tears—they will spoil your make-up.' There was a careful humour in his voice—deliberate, she realised.

She gazed up at him, eyes swimming. His face was a blur. With infinite gentleness he scooped his little finger along the line of her lower lashes, catching the moisture on each before it could run down her cheeks. As her vision cleared his eyes came into focus, looking down into hers.

It was as if she were suspended in time, suspended by the lightest strand of gossamer, the gossamer touch of his fingertip, yet she could no more move, no more breathe, than if she were held in bands of steel.

Everything stopped—her breathing, her heartbeat, so it seemed, and all the world everywhere—just stopped. All that existed was Rafaello, looking down at her, the strangest, most enigmatic expression in his dark, dark eyes.

Her lips parted as the softest exhalation of breath sighed from her.

Slowly Rafaello brushed the tips of his fingers into the fine tendrils of her hair.

'So lovely—'

His voice was a murmur and then his head was lowering to hers, and as Magda's eyes fluttered shut she gave herself to the exquisite wonder of Rafaello di Viscenti, the most beautiful man in the world, kissing her.

His mouth was soft and warm and oh-so-skilful, moving with delicacy, with exploring slowness, tasting her lips as if she were the sweetest dessert.

It went on for an eternity. Yet it was over too soon—achingly soon...

As he drew back from her she felt a loss that echoed through her whole body.

She gazed up at him, her emotions naked on her face.

With that enigmatic expression still in his eyes, Rafaello took her hand and tucked it into the crook of his arm, sliding her dark glasses back over her eyes.

'We must return to the car,' he told her.

She went with him as if she were in a complete daze—because she was. A sort of unreality was enveloping her and she could think no coherent thoughts. Not one.

The journey back to the villa was conducted mostly in silence. Rafaello drove with the speed and total concentration with which he had driven in the morning, but this time there was no aura of anger coming from him. Instead he seemed to be taking particular relish in driving the megapowerful car—and Magda spent the entire journey, head turned towards Rafaello, holding her hair with one hand, as it blew about wildly, and gazing openly at him in utter wonder.

From time to time he glanced across at her, and she saw a little smile playing around his mouth, as if he were pleased, very pleased about something. She didn't know what it was, only that when his mouth indented like that her insides just dissolved all over again.

She wanted the journey never to end.

CHAPTER SEVEN

RAFAELLO was in a good mood. A very good mood. It was the first good mood he'd had for months—ever since his father had given him his impossible ultimatum: marriage or disinheritance.

It made him realise just how bad his sustained mood had been, and for how long.

But all that had changed. The world was smiling again, and he was smiling with it. It was a good, good feeling. A burden had been lifted from his shoulders.

Back at the villa, he received with mixed emotions the news from an expressionless Giuseppe that Enrico had departed for Rome and was not expected back any time soon. Uppermost was, he acknowledged ruefully, relief. In his new improved mood he did not relish any more confrontation, and if his father had decamped to the Rome apartment, well, that was his choice, thought Rafaello. He had better put in a few phone calls to other board members, just to ensure that Enrico was not up to anything so far as his plans for Viscenti AG were concerned, but he was confident enough that his father would not renege on him.

It was with a lighter heart that he turned to Magda.

'Giuseppe tells me my father has gone to stay in Rome— we have an apartment there. Now,' he breezed on, 'why do you not go and see to Benji, hmm?' He smiled at her, and again she felt the butterflies soar on magic wings. 'I must check my e-mails and make some phone calls, but I shall join you soon.'

He strolled off towards the library and Magda, informed by Giuseppe that Benji was asleep upstairs in her room, went upstairs, still in a complete daze.

She wanted desperately to think about what had happened, but Benji was far too pleased, waking from his afternoon nap, to allow time for reverie. His delight at seeing her made her forget everything else, at least for the moment, and she scooped him up and hugged him closely, thanking Gina for her care of him.

Refreshed from his slumber, Benji was ready for action again, and Magda headed downstairs with him.

Maria intercepted her in the hall.

Her eyes gleamed as she took in Magda's transformed appearance, but she said nothing about the new look, merely saying, 'I will bring coffee to the terrace—Signor and Signora Calvi are there.'

So, too, as Magda found, was Benji's new pride and joy—his sit-upon wooden trike on which he could easily push himself along. He fell on it with a cry of glee, and in a short while was racing up and down the paved terrace like a pro. As for Rafaello's aunt, she was decidedly more open about Magda's new appearance.

'Excellent! You look very lovely, my dear—and you will be pleased to hear that the rest of your new wardrobe has been delivered already.'

Magda looked surprised.

'Of course,' said Rafaello's aunt, smiling admonishingly at her expression. 'You cannot survive on one outfit alone. I have inspected the selection and they are all excellent. Gina has already hung them up. Now, come and have a cup of coffee and tell us what you thought of Lucca—and I shall tell you of all the antics of your extremely lively little boy this morning.'

Elizavetta was clearly in a very good humour, and when Rafaello emerged on to the terrace some thirty minutes later he was received in the same tone. But Magda was not blind to the rapid but scrutinising glance she subjected both of them to as he took his seat beside Magda. She felt herself colour slightly. Inside the butterflies set off again as she sipped her coffee, intensely aware of Rafaello's presence beside her as he chatted to his aunt and uncle.

The awareness heightened when, ten minutes later, Rafaello turned to her and said suddenly, 'It is time to cool down—and I am sure Benji would enjoy a swim. Come—'

As he spoke he was aware of a degree of disingenuousness about his invitation. True, he would like to cool down, and probably both mother and child would enjoy a swim, but what he himself would enjoy most would be seeing what Magda looked like in a decent swimsuit.

His thoughts flew back to the previous afternoon, when he'd been surprised to see that, hideously saggy swimsuit apart, she really had a quite unexpectedly pleasing figure. Now, after a morning in Olivia's expert hands, and wearing what he knew would be a beautifully styled piece of swimwear, the results would be, he anticipated, even more pleasing...

His expectations were rewarded. Magda did, indeed, look every bit as good in the sleek peach-coloured one-piece as he had hoped. Cut high in the leg, it emphasised the slenderness of her thighs and hips, her hand-span waist and, most enticingly of all, the gentle swell of her breasts.

Her skin tone had ripened from the Tuscan sun to a warm honey, and with her lovely hair loose over her shoulders as she slowly and self-consciously walked into the pool area, her little boy held by the hand, he could not take his eyes from her.

How had she been hiding all that natural loveliness all this time? He cursed himself for his own blindness—he'd been blinded by that muddy-coloured hair, scraped back, her total lack of attention to her appearance and those atrocious, unspeakable clothes. And now—

Whatever the size of the bill Olivia presented to him, he would have paid it ten times over just for the pleasure of seeing Magda walk towards him now, with her shy, natural grace...

He came near to her. He was all ready for his swim, clad in nothing but his trunks, and he realised from the surge of blood he felt, as powerful as it was instinctive, he would need to get into the water pretty damn fast if those faint stains of colour on her cheeks were not to turn fiery red. Already he could tell she could not cope with his almost nudity—and if her gaze dragged downwards, from where it seemed to be fixated on his torso, then she would have cause to blush indeed!

With a lithe movement he launched himself into the water. The cold had the effect he wanted—for now, at any rate. Several strongly executed lengths later he surfaced to find Magda sitting nervously by the shallow flight of steps leading into the water, Benji already immersed, splashing away mightily. Rafaello hauled himself gracefully and effortlessly out of the water, and reached for Benji's inflatable ball.

'Catch!'

He tossed it towards the little boy, who gave a crow of delight and started to paddle towards the floating ball as fast as his chubby little legs and rubber ring would carry him. He batted at it, and it swirled away, and he chased after it. Magda laughed, and so did Rafaello. He lowered himself into the pool and started to play with the child.

It was, he discovered, extraordinarily easy to entertain an infant. All that was required was a complete lack of dignity and a willingness to engage in a highly repetitious game of throw the ball, throw it again, and again, and again...

'He won't get tired of it before you do,' warned Magda. She was still sitting there, feet in the water, knees pressed together, feeling incredibly, exposingly self-conscious.

Rafaello laughed, and she felt a warmth spreading through her. Her mind was still in a total daze. Could this really be Rafaello di Visenti, who hadn't even wanted to call Benji by name, now playing with him with every sign of pleasure?

And could this really be Rafaello di Viscenti, who had previously looked at her with such disdain, who had looked at her just now, as she'd walked towards him, as if he were unable to take his eyes away from her for a single moment.

I can't take it in—I can't believe this is happening!

If this was nothing but a dream, it was one she never, ever, wanted to wake from.

'So—where would you like to go today?'

Rafaello's voice was inviting. And why not? He was relaxed—more relaxed than he'd been since he could remember, since before his father had started to be fixated upon the idea of him marrying Lucia. He felt, he realised, carefree, with nothing to do but enjoy himself and be pleasurably self-indulgent. Yes, the future of Viscenti AG lay in his hands, and he would take up his responsibilities in due course, but right now global expansion could wait—right now he had another project to pursue.

A very pleasurable one.

He cast a look at the object of his attention.

'Firenze? Pisa? Sienna?'

Magda bit her lip. Rafaello tried not to let his gaze focus on it. There would be time enough for what he intended, but for now the day stretched before them. He wanted to show Tuscany off to Magda—wanted to get her to himself again, truly to himself, without the watching chorus of not just his aunt and uncle but Maria and Giuseppe as well.

'Please,' she said, 'you don't have to show me around—really.'

'It is my pleasure,' he replied airily. 'You have but to choose your destination. How about Firenze? The most magnificent jewel in the crown of Tuscany—whatever the quieter charms of Lucca.'

She smiled, but still looked uncertain.

'Please—don't think me ungrateful, but I feel I cannot leave Benji here—it is not fair either to him, to Maria or your aunt.'

'Then we take him with us.' It was not what he particularly wanted to do, but he could see her point.

Her uncertainty persisted. 'A busy city is perhaps not the best place for him, let alone art museums and historical monuments.'

With a wave of his hand Rafaello disposed of this objection, too. 'The solution is obvious—we'll go to the beach.'

As if he had uttered a magic word, Magda's face lit up. 'Oh, can we really? Benji would adore a beach. He's never been—neither have I…'

Her voice was wistful. Something about it stabbed Rafaello. She had never been to the beach.

But then she had lived such a deprived life—not just in poverty, but with no family. A foundling—abandoned by her mother. Could such things happen? Anger shot through him. No wonder she had clung to this boy from the orphanage, this Kaz of hers. No wonder she had sought comfort in his arms—his bed.

A shadow crossed his eyes. And even that had been taken from her…

'Then it is decided,' he announced decisively. 'The beach it is.'

It was, thought Magda by the afternoon, the best day of her life! Even better than yesterday—for today she had with her both Benji and Rafaello. And Rafaello as she had never yet seen him—as gorgeous as ever, as bewilderingly attentive and approving as yesterday, but as playful as he had been with Benji in the pool at the villa.

And something more as well. She didn't know what the 'more' was, only that it set the blood singing in her veins—

a song that soared to the highest notes whenever she and Rafaello exchanged glances.

She knew she was living in a dream—knew that as she sat on the beach at Viareggio, Benji snug between her out-stretched legs, Rafaello industriously rebuilding the sand-castle that Benji, without fail, would take exuberant plea-sure in demolishing, sun glinting off his golden torso, bronzing his dark silky hair—knew that all she could do was make a memory of the moment.

And she knew, too, how dangerous was the tempting, impossible thought that was seeding itself against all rea-son, all reality, in the deepest part of her—the sweet, utterly unattainable fantasy that she could rewrite reality and be sitting here, not with a man who had married her solely to thwart and insult his father and safeguard his inheritance, but with her true husband, the father of her child...

But they were not a family—no such thing. Rafaello was being kind towards her, that was all. He was just trying to prove wrong the ugly words his father had thrown at her. She felt bad that he was moved to do so. It had hurt, know-ing Rafaello had deliberately chosen her for her undesira-bility, both social and personal, but for herself she did not take shame in it. She was not responsible for her origins, and Benji was a gift from Kaz that she treasured beyond her own life, for whom she would do whatever it took to keep him safe and raise him well. Whether it was working as a cleaner or marrying a stranger who despised her for doing so...

Her eyes flickered to Rafaello again. But he was not despising her now! He was going to great lengths to be kind to her. She felt her heart squeeze.

He caught her gaze, pausing in the act of restoring—yet again—the sandcastle, and as his eyes held hers she felt colour stain her cheeks. He gave her a slow, intimate smile that deepened the colour along her cheekbones. For a long, timeless moment he held her gaze, and what flowed between them made her feel weak.

Benji, sensing distraction, launched himself forward and fell full-length on the castle, demolishing it utterly.

'Oh, Benji, you little monster!' cried Magda, laughing, breaking eye contact with half a sense of relief and half a yearning sense of loss. Rafaello was laughing, too. He climbed to his feet, taking Benji with him in a swinging arc.

'Come,' he told him with mock sternness, 'time to get you wet!' He held a hand down for Magda, and self-consciously she placed hers in his. His grip tightened and he pulled her to her feet. 'You, too!' he told her.

He ran them down to the sea's edge, lapping gently on the sand, and Benji clutched at his hair, infused with laughter. They all collapsed into the water in a splashing heap, and soon Magda was breathless with laughter as Rafaello whooshed Benji in and out of the water, breasting him through the tiny waves while the little boy shouted with pleasure.

Her heart turned over as she stood, legs apart, thigh-deep in water, watching them. Rafaello was so wonderful with Benji. She could not believe it.

Something tugged at her with an emotion that was almost pain. Again the dangerous, tempting thought flitted across her mind—what if this were real? What if they were what the other people on the beach clearly took them for—a family?

She pushed the thought away. Today—this wonderful, heavenly day—was just a memory in the making.

One which would have to last the rest of her life.

It was with a sense of sated happiness that they finally headed back inland at the end of the day. Dreamily she sat beside Benji in the back of the sleek saloon, lost in a haze of sweet contentment. Benji, exhausted and replete with *gelati*, nodded off in his child-seat.

As they wound eastwards along the autostrada, heading for the rolling hills, Magda thought how utterly different this journey was from the one she had made from the airport at the beginning of the week, only four days ago.

Was Rafaello really the same person now as he had been then? She remembered how he had sat, in his corner of the limo, totally absorbed in his work, paying no attention to her or Benji.

We didn't exist for him then, she thought. We were just objects to be used and moved the way he wanted—the way he paid for.

Her eyes shadowed. That last had not changed—he was still paying her. So how did that square with the way he was treating her now? She knew he was being kind to her, but today he really had seemed to be enjoying himself as much as she and Benji. Was that just being kind?

Again, she put the thought aside. There was no point in thinking about it. She would not spoil the sweetness of the day. She would simply sit here, as the powerful car purred along, continue to watch the man who drove, and store up memories.

By the time they reached the villa Magda, too, was nearly asleep. The sun and the sea air had tired her out. Sleepily she extracted Benji, who promptly surfaced with renewed vigour and demanded to be set down. She slid him to his feet and he toddled purposefully towards the door, opened by Giuseppe, who came down to say something to Rafaello and help with the baggage.

'My aunt and uncle have left,' Rafaello said to Magda as he extracted the beach bags from the boot of the car. 'They have gone to console my father in Rome, so Giuseppe tells me. We have the house to ourselves.'

He smiled at her—that same intimate smile he had smiled on the beach. A frisson went through Magda, and a sudden sense of panic as she realised that there would no longer be the reassuring presence of the Calvis over dinner. Last night they had served to dilute the intensity of her awareness of Rafaello, seated at the head of the table and dominating the meal by his presence alone.

Tonight there would be no such buffer. The realisation was alarming.

So when Rafaello said casually, as they went indoors, 'We have been invited out tonight—some friends want to wish me a happy birthday! There will be plenty of time for you to rest and prepare yourself, and put Benji to bed,' her first reaction was relief.

Then, straight away, the implications of what he had just said struck her.

'No, please—you do not have to take me. I will do perfectly well here—' she started.

Rafaello paused and looked at her. 'They also,' he went on, a touch of humour in his face, 'want to take a look at you—they are most curious.'

Magda bit her lip. 'Um—is that wise? I mean,' she went on hastily, 'won't that lead them to think that…that this is a real marriage?'

The words were hard to say, but she had to say them. A strange, unreadable look came into Rafaello's eyes for a moment. Then it cleared. In a bland voice he answered, 'But this *is* a real marriage, Magda—it is quite legal, and we need to behave accordingly. Besides—' a humorous, cajoling note entered his voice '—are you not eager to try out one of your new evening dresses?'

She made no answer, feeling awkward, but Rafaello simply went on smoothly, 'Now, why do you not refresh yourself? Then let Maria have some time with Benji and give him his supper. You can bath him and get him off to sleep, and then get ready for the evening, hmm? Oh…' He paused at the foot of the stairs. 'Maria suggested she root out my old cot—it must be in an attic somewhere—and put it beside your bed. She is anxious, she tells me, that you may roll onto Benji when you are asleep. I trust you do not mind?'

Magda shook her head. 'No—no, of course not. It is very kind of her.'

The cot was already in the bedroom when she went in some moments later with Benji. It was a magnificent affair, well worthy of a di Viscenti, carved and painted, and clearly freshly spring-cleaned by Maria. To her relief, Benji took to it immediately, sitting in it with every sign of complacent possession. Wryly, Magda wondered how fond he'd be of it once it dawned on him that with the wooden side raised and locked into position he would not be able to get out alone. But since it was right up against the high bed she was happy enough for him to try.

It certainly made life easier as she got ready for the evening. Knowing he was safely inside the cot, bathed and ready for sleep, having a last play with his toys, she could go about her ablutions with greater confidence, especially when it came to styling her hair. She had had to wash it after the day at the beach, and was worried she would not be able to recreate the chic style that Olivia's salon had so effortlessly produced. However, she followed the other woman's advice, moussing it a little and then gently blow-drying it with the hairdryer she found in her bedside cabinet.

The effect, when combined with the make-up Olivia had sent, which Magda applied to the best of her ability, was much better than she had hoped. As she stared at herself, at the gently waving mane of hair clouding her shoulders, her kohled eyes huge and her lipsticked mouth lush and vivid, she could not believe such a transformation really was possible.

As Benji, hugging his teddy bear, silky hair smoothed soothingly back from his forehead, sank into a deep sleep,

Magda extracted a long evening gown from the huge antique wardrobe and slipped it on.

It was black, cut on the bias and clung to her hips, and folding softly over her breasts, held up by tiny shoestring straps. She did not need a bra with it; any slight support she needed was built into the bodice. As the fine-grained material slid over her head and shimmered down her slender body she felt its magic begin to work. She walked to the mirror and stared, transfixed.

Wonderingly she touched her throat.

Is this really me?

It seemed impossible—but the reflection staring back at her could not lie. It showed a slender, graceful woman, exquisitely gowned, with her hair in a soft cloud and wide, luminous eyes.

She could not take her eyes from the reflection, staring in wonder at herself.

A soft knock on the door disturbed her reverie. It was Gina, taking over on babywatch.

'Signor di Viscenti is downstairs waiting for you, *signora*,' the girl said, casting an admiring look at Magda's appearance.

Magda picked up a black satin handbag with a discreet designer logo, slipped her feet into the strappy high-heeled shoes, and headed downstairs after bidding Gina goodnight.

As she gingerly descended the wide sweeping stairs, taking careful steps in her narrow long skirt and high, high heels, she realised Rafaello was staring up at her.

She stared back. Her breath caught.

If she had thought Rafaello superb in a business suit, casual clothes and beachwear, in a tuxedo he was, quite simply, breathtaking. The black cloth of the evening jacket stretched tautly across his shoulders, sheathing his torso and providing an ebony contrast to the white dress shirt. He was freshly shaven, freshly showered, his hair still slightly damp as it feathered over his brow. His cheekbones seemed higher than ever, thought Magda, dazzled, and the sculpted line of his mouth could have been hewn by Michelangelo himself...

She went on walking down, eyes fixed on him—and, conscious of him as she was, she was also burningly conscious of how his eyes were fixed on her in return.

As she reached the marble floor he came towards her. Before she could register what he was doing he had lifted her hand and raised it to his mouth.

The graze of his mouth on her knuckles made her want to faint. He straightened his head, but kept her hand in his.

'You look exquisite,' he breathed, his accent stronger than ever, and all she could do was stare up at him, her hand caught in his, her lips parted, her breath stilled.

'You require only one adornment—this.'

His words were accompanied by his slipping his left hand inside his tuxedo jacket and drawing out, not a jewellery case this time, but a sliver of white rainbow. As he opened the palm of his hand Magda could not stop herself giving a gasp.

The necklace was a river of diamonds, fantastic, unbelievable, and as she stared, incredulous, Rafaello simply let go her hand, turned her around, and draped the glittering necklace around her throat, brushing aside her hair to fasten it.

'I can't wear it!' she told him anguishedly. 'I'll lose it.'

He just laughed and turned her back towards him.

She clutched at it around her throat all the way in the car—which Rafaello drove at a pace that was almost sedate.

'I don't want to muss your hair,' he said, and smiled at her, and for a second his gaze held. 'I'm saving that for later,' he murmured, and then, as the road curved, he flicked his gaze back ahead.

Did he really say that...? Magda wondered, thinking she must have misheard. Another thought came to her.

'Rafaello—' it was still strange to say his name; it didn't

come out naturally yet, for all that he was being so nice and kind to her '—what do I need to know about this evening?'

He glanced across at her again, one hand resting lightly on the wheel, the other dipping expertly to change gear and rev up the engine as they rounded a sharp bend in the road.

'Paolo and Sylvia have been married a couple of years—they have one little boy, and Sylvia is expecting her next. I've known Paolo for ever. He'll be curious to know how we ended up together, but don't worry.' He paused minutely to change gear. 'He knows why I've married so suddenly. He's heard action replays of my battles with my father for years.'

Magda swallowed. 'So he knows,' she said awkwardly, 'how you came to select me? And for what reasons?' she added bravely. 'Won't...won't he think it strange that you are taking me with you this evening?'

'No,' he replied tightly.

A sudden new, hideous thought occurred to her. 'You're not...you're not taking me there tonight to...to tell everyone...where...where you found me, are you? Part of...part of your...battle...with your father?'

There was fear in her voice, open and naked. Was that what Rafaello was going to do tonight? Walk her into a room full of strangers and tell them all he'd married a woman who cleaned toilets for a living?

Rafaello swore. Then, with a screech of tyre rubber, he pulled the car over to the side of the road. He turned in his seat.

She was looking at him, stricken, eyes wide, hands twisting in her lap. Something gutted him. She'd looked like that when he'd come out on to the landing to hear his father spill his poison all over her—poison that *he* had fed his father in the first place.

'No!' he said forcefully, then, more gently, 'No—no. This time—' there was irony in his voice, and self-

accusation '—this time I have no such intent. This time…'
His voice changed, and sent a slow quiver along the base
of her spine. 'This time I am taking you with me because—'

His voice cut out. Then, with a twist of wry humour, he
continued, 'Because if I don't then Paolo and Sylvia will
simply turn up tomorrow at the villa to take a look at you.
I thought it would be easier if they met you in the middle
of a party—that way there will be more people around, and
we have the option of leaving whenever we want.'

She was still looking at him, her eyes huge and fearful
in the dim light.

'Don't look scared, *cara*, I will let no harm come to you,'
he told her softly. And then, to chase away that expression,
to stop her looking at him as if she were terrified of the
hurt he could inflict on her—and, he admitted to himself
wryly, to do something he'd been wanting to do since she'd
first walked down the stairs looking so heartbreakingly
beautiful he had not been able to stop staring at her—he
leant across and kissed her.

It was a soft kiss, not passionate—not yet—but a promise. A promise to her. A promise to himself.

His mouth touched hers and she melted into liquid
honey, her eyes fluttering shut as his lips softly moved.
Then he drew back. Her eyes opened again and he was
looking at her, holding her gaze.

'Don't be afraid, *cara*…'

He gunned the engine and pulled out into the road again,
heading off into the dark, headlights cutting a vivid beam
of dazzling brightness through the dark Tuscan night.

The party, Magda discovered, proved no ordeal at all. Quite
the reverse. True, the square Renaissance villa was so op-
ulent, and the driveway so packed with the most expensive,
fantastic cars, that Magda's heart had hammered with

nerves. She couldn't go in! They would all know she wasn't one of them.

As she'd stiffened in fear, an arm had come around her shoulder.

'You look a million dollars—and I will take care of you.'

And he did. Rafaello did not leave her side for a moment, all evening. Not that she needed protection, Magda found. Paolo and Sylvia were welcoming and charming, with a real kindness behind their open curiosity about their friend's unexpected bride. But nothing awkward was asked or said by anyone; everyone simply seemed to accept her at face value.

There was only one tricky moment. About halfway through the evening Sylvia came hurrying over to Rafaello and murmured something urgently to him in Italian. Rafaello merely stilled a moment, then said something dismissive. Sylvia patted his arm approvingly, and disappeared again.

Rafaello turned to Magda. 'Lucia has turned up. Do not be alarmed. She will have no opportunity to insult you.'

But it seemed that insulting the female who had snatched her prospective husband from under her nose was not, after all, Lucia's intention. Instead she glided forward, wearing an excruciatingly figure-hugging gold tissue gown, and her dark eyes widened as she took in the unbelievable transformation of her cousin's wife.

'A Sonia Grasci gown, no less, and diamonds, too! Quite a tribute.'

Her voice was honeyed, but Magda stayed tense. Lucia gave a light laugh.

'Oh, don't look like that. What's done is done. And I don't hold grudges. Besides, it isn't me you have to win over, but Rafaello's father. He was set on me becoming his daughter-in-law.'

There wasn't anything Magda could say to this, and Rafaello simply replied, thought tightened lips, 'My father should have known better than to try and play with my life, Lucia. And now, if you will excuse me, we must circulate.'

He whisked Magda away and promptly introduced her to yet more friends who, like everyone else, seemed to see nothing exceptional about her—only that she had arrived so suddenly on the scene.

Only one was bold enough to comment on it—and on Lucia's disappointed expectations.

Rafaello merely smiled silkily. 'As you can see—' he pulled Magda a little more closely to him to make his point '—I was busy elsewhere.'

The other man grinned. 'So that's why you were forever disappearing to London!'

Rafaello's smile deepened. 'Who could blame me?' he murmured, as if confirming the other man's assumption that his acquaintance with his English bride was long standing.

Magda's breathlessness at being held so close to him precluded any possibility of her saying a word.

As they circulated yet again, Rafaello, who did not relinquish his hold on her, with a continuing effect on Magda's ability to speak coherently, paused and looked down at her.

'Enjoying yourself?' he asked.

She nodded dumbly. Then managed to say, 'Everyone is very nice.'

He smiled indulgently. 'You are being much admired,' he went on.

Magda coloured. 'It's very kind of you to say so,' she answered quietly.

He gave a laugh. 'Kind? Is that what you think, *cara*? I can see I shall have to persuade you otherwise.'

He looked down at her, and there was something in his eyes that made her breath catch.

They did not stay much longer. Magda had no idea what time it was, but soon they were climbing into Rafaello's car, being bade farewell by Paolo and Sylvia. Both, she saw, had knowing smiles on their faces.

Rafaello caught her embarrassed expression as he started the engine.

'They know we are newly-weds,' he said. 'We are being permitted to leave early on that account.'

'Oh,' said Magda, and busied herself with her seat belt.

The journey back seemed to take no time at all. Perhaps, thought Magda, it was the result of the champagne singing in her bloodstream.

Back at the villa, as Rafaello helped Magda out of the car, her heel caught on the gravel slightly. The steadying arm that Rafaello put around her shoulder seemed to invite her to lean back into him, finding that she fitted very snugly against the smoothness of his tuxedo jacket. They walked indoors.

'Do you want to check on Benji?' Rafaello asked. 'I expect Gina will be glad to go off duty.'

'Oh—yes,' she answered. She headed upstairs, carefully gathering the narrow skirt of her dress in one hand, conscious of Rafaello's regard as she ascended.

In her room, having thanked and said goodnight to Gina, she went to gaze at Benji, fast asleep in his lordly cot. Gently she dropped a silent kiss on his forehead, her heart filled with love for him, then turned away, unfastening the diamonds at her throat.

A sadness seemed to fill her at knowing the evening was over. More than sadness—a restlessness she could not name. On impulse she pulled back the heavy curtains and opened the window. She leant against the sill, chin on the heels of her hands, gazing out, letting the warm night air sift over her face, scented with flowers.

She gave a little sigh. The shadowed garden, shot with a dim pool of light from her own window and one, she assumed, from Rafaello's, beyond hers, spread mysteriously below. The sounds of the night came soft to her ears.

She gave another little sigh. She had nothing to be sad about, she knew. Tonight had been magical and its memory would be treasured for ever, along with every other moment she had spent with Rafaello di Viscenti. Wanting him so much and knowing she would never have more of him than she had now. He was not for her, nor she for him, however beautiful he made her feel...

'That, I should inform you, *cara*, is a very dangerous position for you to be in.'

CHAPTER EIGHT

THE deep voice behind her was a drawl, shot with humour—and something more. Magda started, drawing back and straightening up, turning towards him.

'I...I won't fall out,' she protested.

Rafaello sauntered towards her, hands in his trouser pockets. He must have emerged from the bathroom, through the previously locked adjoining door. Though he still wore his tuxedo jacket he had loosened his tie, and it hung on either side of his undone top shirt button. Magda felt her insides turn over.

'That was not the danger I referred to,' he corrected her. 'It was this.'

He closed in on her. A hand slid around her back and spanned her derrière.

'It was projecting far too temptingly,' he murmured down at her.

There was a light in his eye that made her insides churn again.

'Rafaello—' she gasped faintly, trying to draw away from him. But that only made the warm, devastating pressure on her rear increase. As if unwilling to tolerate her escape, he simply pulled her closer against him, moving his hand upwards into the small of her back and curving his other hand beneath the cloud of her hair to hold the nape of her neck.

She had no breath in her. No breath to speak, to protest, to exclaim—or even to breathe.

Rafaello smiled down into her face.

'There is only one way,' he told her softly, 'to end an evening like this.'

His head lowered to hers, and closed over her breath-lessly parted lips.

He started to kiss her.

It had happened so suddenly she had had no time, no chance, to do or say anything. One moment she had been gazing out of the window into the Tuscan night, thinking the evening was over, and the next Rafaello had closed in on her and was making love to her.

Because that was what he was doing—making love to her mouth, his lips brushing over hers, moistening and lav-ing, teasing them apart with his, sensually, devastatingly, to open her to him and take his fill of her.

She was lost, so completely lost that the roof could have caved in and she would not have noticed. His fingers speared into her hair, kneading at her scalp. His other hand slipped down over the soft mound of her bottom, and did likewise to the silk-covered flesh there.

Sensation shot through her body like fireworks. His kisses were deepening, her mouth was fully open to him now, and his tongue was meeting hers, tasting and mating. The blood pounded in her veins, her ears, and of their own volition her hands wrapped over his hard, lean spine and held him close, crushing his torso against her breasts which suddenly, extraordinarily, felt full and swollen.

He was murmuring something into her mouth, but she could make no sense of it. Could make no sense of any-thing, only go on, and on, kissing and being kissed.

Then his arm was around her waist, his hand at her shoulder, though his mouth never left hers, and he was urging her forward.

'My bed,' she heard him say, and his voice was a husk.

She found her voice, dragged it up from the depths.

'Rafaello—please—I...I...'

'Hush,' he said into her mouth. 'Hush—it will be good—this is right for us, *cara*—trust me. I want you so much...'

His kiss deepened again and almost, almost she gave

herself to it totally, gave herself to everything he was offering, everything she had never dared even dream about.

But dreams were not real—and this was not reality. It could not be. It must not be.

She dragged her mouth away again, halting as he swept her forward.

'Rafaello—no. Please—please listen to me—you don't understand—'

He heard the plea in her voice and let her draw away, but only so far as he could still hold her in the circle of his arms. His dark eyes searched hers in the low light.

'Don't be afraid—I will not hurt you. I know it has been a long time for you, and that losing Benji's father so tragically was hard—unbearable. But you must move on, embrace life again.'

Her eyes had widened at his words and she seemed to be trying to speak, but he would not let her.

'You are a beautiful, desirable woman—a whole new life is opening to you now. The past is gone—remember Kaz for the son he gave you, but now embrace life again.'

There was consternation in her face now, and her mouth worked until words came.

'Kaz? No—you don't understand—Kaz wasn't Benji's father,' she said faintly.

He stilled, as if she had struck him. 'Then who—?' He frowned—what was happening?

She felt his arms around her slacken, and drew back.

'I…I don't know.'

His face darkened. *'Come?'*

She swallowed. 'I don't know who Benji's father is. You see—'

He stepped away. Tension was in every line of his body.

'You do not *know* who fathered him?'

There was a haunted look in her eyes, but he ignored it. Inside he felt a slow-burning fuse of anger ignite.

'You have been with so many men you do not know which one got you pregnant?'

The biting harshness of his words flayed her. He could see she looked stricken, appalled, but he struck again. 'So this Kaz you spoke of—this tragic loss—is just a sob story—to soften me?'

She took another step backwards. 'You don't understand,' she whispered.

His mouth twisted. 'Oh, I understand, all right. I understand the truth now. I thought to defend you—to prove that my insults were untrue! But however misfortunate your life there is no excuse—none—for indulging in promiscuity so great that you could not even be bothered to choose a single father for your child.' Disgust filled his face. 'Did you never stop to consider the effect of your total irresponsibility upon an innocent child? Are you yourself not living proof of the fruits of such irresponsibility? And yet you do it again, to your own son.'

'Benji has *me*!' she cried anguishedly. 'I will never leave him, *never*!'

His face stilled.

'A boy needs a father.'

There was something in his voice that was bleak.

'A boy needs a father,' he said again. 'And you have deliberately deprived your son of that right—he will not even know who his father was! Or will you lie to him and tell him this Kaz of yours fathered him? To shield him from the truth of what his mother was?'

His voice was scornful, condemning. Angrily he strode across the room, heading for the bathroom and his own room beyond. He felt gutted, as though something wonderful, something rare and surprising, had just turned to mildew in his hands.

As she watched him go Magda stood, reeling. From passion to fury in a few moments. She felt winded. But she also knew that she had to go after him.

She reached the communicating door just as he was about to shut it, and held her hand out to halt him.

'Rafaello,' she said, in a low, unsteady voice, 'I don't know who fathered Benji, it's true. And I know that depriving a child of its father is a terrible thing to do—but…but…please make allowances for Kaz.'

His face darkened.

'Kaz? You just said he was not Benji's father.'

Magda swallowed. 'It's true. Kaz wasn't Benji's father. Kaz…' She hesitated, then said it. 'Kaz was Benji's mother.'

He stared at her as if she had run mad. She forced herself to go on.

'Kaz was like a sister to me. We only ever had each other in all the world. When…when the cancer came back she went…a little mad, I think. She knew she was going to die before she had even begun to live. And she told me…she told me…' There was a tight steel band constricting her throat, making it impossible to breathe, to talk, but she forced herself on. 'She told me that if she couldn't live, if she was going to be wiped out as if she had never existed, then she wanted…wanted to prove that she *had* existed—that if *she* couldn't live she would leave a part of herself behind. Was it so wrong?' Her voice was a whisper. 'Was it so wrong for her to conceive a child any way she could, to leave something of herself behind? How could I tell her no? How *could* I, when I wasn't facing what she was facing? All I could do was promise to raise her child and be the mother she was not going to be allowed to be. She knew I would never abandon Benji—*never*—because I had been abandoned myself. She knew she could trust me with him. So she gave him to me, just before…just before she died.'

The tears were rolling down her cheeks now, unstoppable, as the memories of her friend came crowding back. She stood there, her hand against the door, and could say nothing more.

Then arms came around her, strong and protecting, and gathered her up, and the tears flowed and flowed. She could hear Italian being murmured, but all she could tell of it was the comfort in his voice as she clung to him.

It took a long while for the tears to stop. In the early months, when she had still been raw from Kaz's death, with Benji still so tiny, so bereaved, they had come often, in the loneliness of the night, but it had been a long, long time since she had cried—and never with anyone to comfort her.

At last there were no more tears. Rafaello slipped his arm around her shoulder and led her into his room. 'Sit,' he said, and there was a gentleness in his voice she'd never heard before. He lowered her down to an armchair beside the empty fireplace and hunkered down beside her. He took her hands.

'Forgive me for my anger at you—I spoke in ignorance.' His mouth twisted wryly. 'As I have done before about you.' He paused a moment. 'I have only one thing to say— that Benji is a fortunate child to have such devotion from you.'

'He is my son.' It was a cry from her heart.

Rafaello pressed her hands. 'He is your son,' he confirmed. 'And your love for him shines like a beacon in the dark. You have taken him into your heart, and he is there for ever now.'

He raised her hands to his lips. Something was singing inside him—something that sounded a sweet, clear note. He stood up, taking her with him, still holding her hands.

And then, in the dim light, he kissed her.

It was a light kiss, as soft as silk, but when he kissed her again, holding her hands against his chest so that she could feel the warmth of his body through the palms of her hand and the fine material of his shirt, his embrace deepened.

'I desire you very much,' he told her softly. 'Will you stay with me tonight?'

Her eyes were deep and dark.

'Rafaello—I…there is something you should know—'

He smiled. 'You have more secrets?' he chided. 'Tell me all!'

She felt herself colour slightly. 'A moment ago you thought me promiscuous and you were angry—'

He shook his head. 'My anger was at the thought of your irresponsibility in conceiving a child who could not name his father. But,' he acknowledged, 'as for promiscuity itself—well, I have known many women—perhaps I should not have, but…' he met her eyes with a rueful look '…it came easily to me. Do not think me too conceited, but a man with money is always attractive.'

'Especially if he looks like you,' Magda found herself answering with her own little tug of a smile.

'If I agree you will definitely think me conceited,' he answered, with a faint, wry smile. 'But, whatever the cause, I am therefore hardly in a position to criticise you if you are as experienced as I am.'

'Yes, but the thing is,' she replied, embarrassed, dipping her head so she wouldn't have to look him in the eye, however dim the light was, 'I'm not experienced at all.'

Her words fell into a pool of silence. Then, wordlessly, he put her away from him, letting slip her hands.

'That's why I said about Kaz not being Benji's father when you said I should not hold back for Kaz's sake,' she went on, feeling mortified now. 'I knew—I knew you would obviously assume that I had at least sufficient experience to have become pregnant, but in fact I…I don't have any experience. None. Never.'

Her voice trailed off and she wished, oh, just wished, she could disappear down a crack in the floor.

'You are a virgin?' There was something odd in his voice. She didn't know what it was, she just wanted that crack to widen, so she could slip away through it, boring, unexciting, inexperienced reject that she was. She should have remembered that Cinderella returned to her rags at midnight. Of no interest whatsoever to a sophisticated, worldly, experienced man like Rafaello di Viscenti.

'I'm sorry,' she said miserably.

'You are sorry?' There was that odd note in his voice again. She stared down at the floor, her fingers twisting in the fabric of her skirts.

Then, suddenly, he had stepped towards her again, and his long, cool fingers were sliding either side of her jaw, tilting her face up towards him.

'Don't you know,' he said softly, 'that there is only one thing to be done with a virgin?'

She gazed at him, her breath catching. He was just so perfect—his dark, beautiful eyes, his silky black hair, his sculpted, sensual mouth...

'Seduce her...' he breathed. 'Take her body...' His fingers slipped into the softness of her hair, teasing the delicate border between her cheek and the graceful fall of hair, touching, oh, so lightly, the lobes of her ears. 'Take her body touch by touch, by touch...' His fingers drifted along the line of her jaw, the length of her throat, with such feathering lightness she thought she must die of it. 'Kiss...by kiss...by kiss.' Each word was murmured against her eyes, fluttering shut, the corner of her mouth. 'Until you have taken her with you on that most perfect journey of all...'

His mouth grazed hers, and she lifted her face to him like a flower, drinking in his nectar.

'Will you come with me, *cara*, on that journey? Will you let me take you there?' He was kissing her as he spoke, light, seductive kisses that she could no more resist than a snowflake melting on a warm cheek. There were only two people in the entire world—herself and Rafaello di Viscenti, the most beautiful man she had ever seen. His hands were framing her face, his fingers teasing, his mouth caressing hers with exquisite, feathered lightness. But beneath the lightness a hunger was growing. She could feel it, building in her veins, her head, making her mouth answer his, taste him as he was tasting her, dissolving the world around her into nothing more than exquisite, honeyed sensation.

She wanted it never to stop, but for all that it was not enough—it was feeding its own hunger, its own yearning.

Her body pressed itself against his, a slender wand against his lean hardness, her palms caught between her breasts and his chest.

She gave a little moan, deep in her throat, as he teased open her mouth, releasing yet more and more sensation, until she felt flame flickering throughout her body. She felt her breasts quicken, swelling against him, and the sensation was as wondrous as it was arousing.

Time slipped away, lost in sensation. There was nothing, nothing but this. Nothing but the touch of his fingers at her shoulders, slipping the tiny shoestring straps over the cusp of each arm, and gently, oh, so gently, his hands warm on her flanks, sliding the silky material of her dress down the slender column of her body. He was kissing her all the while, but as the dress pooled at her feet he let her go and stepped back.

She stood there, the dark material spread on the floor, her body bathed in the soft light from the low lamps. Her instinct was to cover her breasts, but instinct was fighting with another impulse, yet more powerful—to stand quite still and let Rafaello's eyes drink in the sight of her as a thirsty man would drink purest spring water. So she stood, one slender silk-clad leg taking slightly more weight that the other, the tiny line of her wisp of panties around her narrow hips, her eyes huge and liquid as she displayed herself to him.

'*Bellissima…*' His voice was low, and husked. 'Beautiful—so beautiful…'

Her heart soared. To hear such a word on his lips was a pleasure so sweet, so melting she could not believe it.

'Am I?' Her words were a whisper.

'Do you doubt it?' His hand reached out and slowly, with infinite delicacy, his fingers traced around the swelling aureole of her breast. It flowered beneath his touch, and a shiver of pleasure went through her, a trembling in all her limbs. His fingers moved to her other breast and performed the same office there.

'Bellissima,' he said again. Then his hand slipped to hers and, folding her fingers in his own, he led her towards the bed.

It was a dream, thought Magda—it had to be a dream. Reality this wondrous, this magical, could never exist. Yet how could it be a dream? The touch of Rafaello's hands was upon her body, laying her down upon the cool sheets. Pausing only to swiftly shed his own clothes—making her first gaze in adoration at the lean, dark revelation of skin and sinew, muscle and smooth, smooth flesh, making her lashes wash blushingly down over her eyes as her gaze worked downwards from his torso—he came and half lay beside her, lowering his head to kiss, not her lips, but those swelling, aching orbs that yearned again for his arousing caress.

She felt her spine arch, lifting her breasts towards him, and her hands reached for him, her fingers stroking into his dark, silky hair. A sigh of bliss eased from her as his tongue and lips suckled her, laving her nipples, one after the other, again and again, until sweetness was flooding through her.

Yet for all the sweetness, all the bliss, she wanted more. Bliss was feeding bliss, arousing her yet more and more, and a strange, yearning aching was spreading through her body, through every vein, every nerve, making her strain towards him.

He lifted his head from her. His eyes were dark pools, pupils dilated.

'You must take this journey slowly, *cara mia*, the first time. It cannot be hurried, this first flowering of your body.

And the waiting…' a slow, sensual smile played over his parted lips as he dropped his voice '…is part of the journey.'

As he spoke he moved his fingers to the soft underside of her breasts, grazing them. Then he let them trail downwards, across the flat planes of her abdomen, smoothing along her flanks before drifting inwards to tease at the central dip of her belly button. But even as his forefinger circled there the spread of his hand spanned the vee of her legs, and all at once, instantly, achingly, she became aware, for the very first time in her life, of the low, insistent throb that had started up.

Did she give a little moan? She did not know, could not tell. Could only tell that now his forefinger was moving slowly, tantalisingly along the dark band of her panty waist, back and forth, while the throb between her legs intensified and the aching, yearning feeling became yet more and more insistent.

He cupped the mound at her vee, and the sudden pressure of the heel of his hand made her gasp, head rolling. He pressed again, and then his other hand was at her throat, spanning upwards to her jaw, holding her still while his body moved over hers.

As his mouth came down she opened to him eagerly, and the weight of his body seemed glorious and possessive. For a long, endless moment he kissed her passionately, his tongue forging deep within her, mating with hers, and she responded, excitement flaring within her like a hot crimson flame. Then, just as suddenly, he withdrew from her.

'Ah, Magda *mia*.' His voice was rueful. 'I betray my own promise and become greedy for you myself.'

As of itself, her mouth reached up for his. 'I don't mind,' she said huskily, and tried to catch his lips as her hands curled around his shoulders to draw him down to her again.

But he lifted his head further back and smiled crookedly. 'No. This first time is a dish to savour slowly—afterwards—ah, well…' his voice rasped '…then we shall see…' A deep, shuddering breath went through him as he steadied himself, and for the first time Magda registered that part of the hard, masculine weight resting on her was very, *very* masculine…

Her eyes widened in recognition of the fact, and as if he could read her thoughts that crooked, rueful smile came again. 'I must be gentle with you, *cara*, and feast upon you…slowly.'

His voice dropped on the last word and sent a shiver of anticipation through her. His smile became sensual, his eyes speaking.

'There are pleasures, my sweet one, in making love in many ways. As I will show you…'

As he spoke his hand, which had been holding her hip, gentled, and began to slide down her thigh. As it encountered the embroidered top of her stockings he gave a mock frown.

'What is this?' he demanded softly.

He did not wait for an answer. Instead he started to slide the silky fabric downwards, his fingers, as he did so, grazing deliciously along the tender flesh of her inner thigh. It was like having warm honey poured over her, she thought, and her mind dissolved into bliss. She felt her body relax into the bedclothes, lose the urgent tension of the past few moments, when it had been consumed by a need she could not name.

Now she needed nothing, nothing in all the world, except this most exquisite sensation of Rafaello's hands sliding her stocking down her leg. When he reached the end, and flicked it aside, he returned to pay attention to her other stocking. His fingers played with the embroidered top, and as they grazed along her inner thigh she felt her legs part a little, falling open slightly. The delicious, exquisite sensation of his taking the stocking off her came again, pouring warm honey over every millimetre of skin. She sank back into the deep, soft bedclothes, her eyes fluttering shut, giving herself to the sensation.

And then, as the second stocking was flicked aside, she felt his hands drifting back up her leg again. But this time when he reached the top of her leg his fingers went on, grazing along the tender flesh of her inner thigh, relaxed and open now, as she lay abandoned to him, and began to brush with tiny, insidious strokes closer and closer to the satin edge of her panties.

The sensation was exquisite—if she had thought his touch on her thighs exquisite she had known nothing, *nothing*! A soft little moan came from her throat as his forefinger came to rest on the plumped satin cupping the curling nest beneath. Warm honey melted through her again, and as his finger began its minute circling movements she realised that it was not just the sensation of melting honey that was flooding through her—her own body was responding to his intimate touch. She seemed liquid, molten, and as the sensation became almost unbearable he intensified it almost beyond endurance. His head lowered to her breast again, his tongue laving softly at the aureole, until her whole body felt like a warm, liquid flame.

Then his fingers were picking at the skimpy waistline of her panties, shushing them down over her hips, sliding them down her parted legs and casting them aside with her stockings.

And then they returned to where she ached for them to be.

It was bliss, bliss beyond imagining, beyond dreams. Her body moved beneath his hand, his mouth, and she felt that warmth flooding through her more sweetly yet, more yearningly still, until every fibre, every nerve ached with wanting.

With agonising slowness his fingers explored her silky folds, eliciting yet more and more pleasure, until she was faint with it.

'Rafaello...' Her voice was weak—weak with longing, weak with desire. She wanted, oh, she wanted... She did not know. But the desire, the need for it was all-consuming. The need for him...him...to join with her, possess her...

'Rafaello...' It was a plea, abject and full of desire. Her hands had found his body, sliding across his shoulders, his back, glorying in the muscled silk of his skin, wanting to draw him down upon her, to draw him into her...

She was flooding—flooding with moisture and desire. The flame of her body was twisting, aching, the sensations at her breast, her body's core, crescendoing, wanting.

'Rafaello—' she said again, and this time, this time his mouth came from her breast and plundered hers instead, kissing her deeply, oh, so deeply, that she gave another moan in her throat and fed upon him as he fed upon her. Then he was moving over her, his fingers loosing from her, steadying himself, his thighs warm and heavy on hers, holding himself above her as for one last, exquisitely tormenting moment his finger centred on the tiny, swollen bud, vibrating it until the warm flame that was her body suddenly, blissfully, seared into incandescence.

The sheet of liquid fire spread out from her ignited core and she gasped with delight and disbelief, for how could such bliss, such ecstasy be possible? And as she did her body opened to him and he was drawn into her, piercing and filling her as her convulsing muscles widened around him and took him into her.

There was pain, but it was fleeting, pushed out by the tide of ecstasy flooding through her, and she cried out, arms wrapping around him urgently.

He filled her absolutely, and as her virgin muscles stretched around him the waves of bliss seemed to intensify, and she cried out again, and again, into the warmth and hunger of his mouth.

'Yes,' he soothed her. 'Yes. Yes, my beautiful girl.'

She did not hear him, could not hear him. Could only

feel. Her whole body was sensation, wonderful, unutterable sensation, which went on and on, ceaseless and without end.

He took her every centimetre of the way, urging her on with subtle movements of his body, with the kisses of his mouth, the urging of his hands on her flanks as the tide of bliss took her on to the very end of her journey.

To leave her there, exhausted, sated, disbelieving, in the shelter of his arms.

He smoothed the hair from her face, smiling down at her, and she felt her heart melt as her body had done, into warm, honeyed flame. A sweetness she had never known filled her heart and soul.

'Rafaello…' Her voice slurred, but her eyes shone with a luminescence that drank him in.

'Cara?' he said, and kissed her softly.

Her heart was racing, and she could feel its pulse in her throat, her wrists.

'Thank you…' she breathed.

The smile came again. 'It was my pleasure,' he told her. 'And yours, I think.'

His long-lashed gaze washed over her. He knew exactly what she had felt, what she had experienced.

'Oh, yes!' she answered on a rapturous exhalation. 'Oh, yes…'

His mouth quirked. 'And tell me, my beautiful little virgin-no-more, would you like to feel that way again?'

Her eyes widened incredulously, and he laughed softly. 'Did you think such pleasure comes only once? For you…' his voice took on a rueful, envious tinge '…there is no limit. But for me—' his voice changed '—I can wait no longer—'

He began to move within her, and Magda, eyes widening in her ignorance of such matters, realised with a shock that he was still as full and strong within her as he had ever been. He registered her reaction and smiled again—but this time there was something wolfish in his smile.

'Do not be anxious, *bellissima mia*, you shall come with me, be assured.'

He was as good as his word. As he lifted himself to stroke within her she felt a surge of pleasure shaft through her. She caught her breath, astonished at her sated body's quick recovery. He moved within her, deeper yet, and when she felt the walls of her body resist, suddenly they yielded again.

She clutched him more tightly, clenching her muscles around him, simultaneously tightening her arms around his back.

He gave his wolfish smile again. 'More?'

The expression in her eyes gave him the answer he expected, and he obliged her yet again. But with every stroke she could see, though her body was starting to focus purely on its own renewed pleasure, that this was as good for him as it was for her.

He stroked again, and again, and again, and with each stroke the surge of excitement thrust through her. She clutched at his back, feeling the skin dampen as the pace of his lovemaking increased. There was an urgency to him now, and she joined him, as eager for him to find his pleasure as she was to find hers again. Their bodies moved in unison, her hips rising to meet his thrusts, her head thrown back, feeling with each urgent, pulsing stroke that she was coming nearer, nearer to something, something…

Something that crested like a deep ocean wave, crested and then thundered through her, shocking her with its intensity, a surging, powerful breaker that caught her and plunged her into a maelstrom of overpowering sensation, seeming to roll her over and over, tumbling her, limbs threshing, muscles convulsing, sensation bucking through her, carrying her on and on and on…

She lay in utter exhaustion, supine beneath him, and realised dimly that his dead weight was pressing down upon her, the full length of his body. His heaviness was total, his limbs completely inert. For a long, timeless while they lay together, still one but both cast away on the furthest shore.

She was tired, infinitely tired. Slowly, heavily, her arms fell from his back, collapsing on to the sheets. Her eyes sank shut and she breathed in the scent of his body as sleep took her.

CHAPTER NINE

SHE awoke, it seemed, an aeon later. As she eased into consciousness her first thoughts were confused. Where was she? Where was Benji? Why hadn't he woken her as he always did? Panicked, she hauled herself upright and blinked, even more disorientated as she stared around at the strange bedroom. And then total, absolute memory flooded through her, and at the same time she became aware of a dull, strained ache between her legs. But more pressing matters asserted themselves.

'Benji!' she cried out in alarm, and as if he had simply been waiting for her call at that moment Rafaello sauntered into his bedroom via the adjoining bathroom, carrying Benji. Seeing her, both broke into smiles, Benji immediately reaching out his arms for her. Rafaello—clad only, Magda became immediately aware, in a pair of jeans—crossed to the bed, bared torso very clearly on display, and lowered Benji down to her.

'Maria has given him his breakfast and got him clean and dressed.' His eyes swept down over her. 'You were tired, *cara*, and I let you sleep.'

Magda bent her head, feeling heat stealing into her cheeks, and busied herself embracing an enthusiastic Benji. But as soon as he had reassured himself of his mother's presence he climbed off her and started to burrow under the bedclothes. Magda wished she could do the same. Looking Rafaello in the eye right now was not something she felt she could do.

'Shy, *cara*?' he enquired softly, recognising her reaction.

He found it enchanting. Swiftly, Rafaello's mind worked back, trying to recall any similar instances of past partners greeting him in the morning with a becoming flush, down-cast eyes and a general air of shy confusion. There were none.

All his previous women had been highly sexually confident females, knowing full well their own attractions. He couldn't imagine any of them ever having been shy about going to bed with him—or anyone.

Magda was a million miles away from any of his previous women.

And not just because of her virginity. Or her shyness.

Just *what* it was about her that made her so different he couldn't work out yet.

But he'd find out.

He lowered himself to the bed, noting with inner humour how she automatically jerked her legs away from him beneath the bedclothes. Placing his hands on the mattress either side of her thighs, he leant forward.

'*Buon giorno,*' he said invitingly, his eyes gleaming softly.

She didn't seem to know what he wanted, so he showed her.

A soft kiss of greeting, just brushing her tender mouth and then withdrawing. As he drew back he saw her flush had mounted, and she still could not meet his eye.

He smiled, and saw her gaze flicker momentarily to his.

'There is no need for shyness, *cara*. You are a woman now.'

Yes, he thought, and I have made her so. An amazing feeling swept through him at the realisation. It was quite extraordinary. She was transformed from that poor, scrawny, unlovely creature whom no man would look at once, let alone twice, into something…someone….who would turn heads wherever she went.

A strange sensation moved inside him. He did not know what it was—it was something he had never felt before, and he wondered at it. His eyes swept over her again, looking at him so shyly, so uncertainly—and yet with a hunger in her eyes for him that he was sure she did not realise was blazing through her embarrassment. The hunger he recognised, for it mirrored his own. He started to lower his head to hers again. She looked so *good*, lying back against his pillows, even if the bedclothes were clutched up to her chin. He reached forward with a hand, meaning to draw them off her so that he could see her lovely, delicate body in the warm morning light. And more than see...

A head pushed itself out from under the bedclothes by his elbow and a tiny hand landed plumply on his, where it pressed into the mattress bearing the weight of his inclining torso. A gurgle of infant laughter burst out of Benji as he crowed at his achievement, emerging from his hiding place.

Rafaello sat back, wry resignation in his face. There would be no lovemaking this morning, he could tell. Immediately he started thinking how swiftly he could convey Benji into Maria's care, so that he could get Magda to himself again.

But not yet, it seemed. Benji wanted to play. Especially with this interesting new addition to morning playtime. He crawled across to Rafaello and deposited himself on his lap, chuckling and making jigging movements to encourage him.

'He wants you to bounce him on your knees,' said Magda, finding her voice at last. At least talking about Benji was possible—he was a safe, neutral subject, and nothing, nothing whatsoever to do with what Rafaello had been talking to her about—which, right now, she couldn't cope with—not at all, not in the slightest.

'Like this?' enquired Rafaello, and twisted round so that he was sitting at right angles, with his feet on the floor again.

'Yes. You hold him on and play "This is the way the lady rides",' explained Magda helpfully.

She ran through the game with him, explaining how the

lady rode very timidly, and the gentleman rode very solemnly, but then the farmer rode with a huge and exaggerated bumpety-bump which reduced Benji to peals of laughter.

And Rafaello, too. Magda watched him repeat the game at least five times for Benji, and her heart simply turned over and over in her chest. He looked so *beautiful*, with his smooth, lean torso, not an ounce of fat on him, his strong arms holding Benji firmly but with such care, and oh, his face, his face, with its sculpted planes and laughing mouth, and his dark, beautiful eyes crinkling at the corners, and his dark, silky hair flopping over his forehead...

Her heart went on turning and turning and turning...

She felt so happy she thought she must die.

But not so happy that she wasn't still filled to the brim with total, absolute shyness about what had happened.

Thank goodness Benji was there! After the fifth repetition she lifted him from Rafaello, taking great pains not to actually touch the man who had swept her to paradise last night, terrified that if she did it would immediately be obvious to him that what she longed for right now was for him to sweep her there all over again.

'That's quite enough, you little monster.' She nuzzled affectionately at Benji. 'It's time to get up.'

She was about to throw the bedclothes aside and stand up when she realised with a flush that she had not a stitch on. She froze.

Rafaello took pity on her. He got to his feet.

'I'll take Benji downstairs. We'll be on the terrace. Come and have your breakfast there with me.'

He scooped Benji from her, taking far less pains than Magda against touching as he did so, and she felt her skin quiver where his fingers brushed her bare arms as she transferred Benji to him. Only when he had definitely left the room did she dare get out of bed and dart through into the bathroom.

She stopped short, seeing her reflection in the bathroom mirror.

It was her body—and yet not her body. She stood, gazing, seeing the fullness of her breasts which surely had not been there before. There was a curve to her hip, too, and—this she was definitely not imagining!—there were soft, lip-shaped discolorations on her throat and breasts. As if in answer to her own thoughts she became aware of the dull throbbing between her legs.

It really happened, she thought, her eyes gazing at her reflection in amazed wonder. It really happened...

That deep, quivering flush of happiness suffused her again, at its core a wonder and a piercing ache that made her feel her heart was opening. A slow, blissful smile lit her face. Whatever happened, whatever happened to her the rest of her life, she would have this moment—this wonderful, blissful, unbelievable moment—when the most beautiful man in the world had taken her to his bed and made a woman out of her.

Despite the residual soreness that remained from the physical experience of that transition, she showered and dressed on winged feet, filled with an overpowering longing to be in his company again. She did not know what the day would bring—what any part of the future would bring. She only knew that now, right now, she just wanted to be with Rafaello, feel his presence, and drink him in like a glass of golden champagne.

On the terrace Rafaello was waiting for her. As she approached his eyes lit with an assessing look, and she immediately became super-conscious of the way the beautifully cut pale blue sundress she had not been able to resist putting on from the huge selection that now crowded her wardrobe moulded her breasts and hips.

She took her place and occupied herself pouring out coffee. Benji glanced at her briefly from astride his new trike before zooming off along the terrace.

Rafaello leant towards her. His bare chest was like polished steel in the bright morning light.

'Well, *cara*, what would you like to do today, hmm?'

He might have been asking her as a tourist, but the expression in his eyes made it perfectly clear what he wanted her answer to be. She felt the colour run up her cheeks again.

'Um, whatever you like,' she answered confusedly. Then went on hurriedly, 'But don't you have to go into the office or something?'

Rafaello shook his head. 'I can think of nothing more tedious,' he answered.

And it was true. The very thought of sitting at his desk, expanding di Viscenti AG into a global empire, was the most boring idea in the world. No, his world today was centred here—on this extraordinarily enticing woman.

Benji came roaring back in true Formula One style, and as Rafaello glanced at him he felt himself still.

She had taken on another woman's son to raise as her own. A dying woman had trusted Magda with her own child...

He felt something constrict inside him. What did it take, he thought, to do such a thing? It was a choice that had cost her so much in material terms. For the sake of her dying friend she had taken on a newborn baby, with no support other than what the state provided—no family, barely any money, not even a home of her own to raise him in. But she had done it—turned herself into a drudge, living in penury, because she would not turn her back on a helpless baby who had no one else to look after him.

Emotion surged through him.

Thank God I found her!

He had taken her away from all that poverty-stricken drudgery, brought her here and released her, like a bird from her cage, to fly on iridescent wings in the summer's warmth. Well-being flooded through him, and something more—something more...

A hand planted on his knee drew his attention. Benji wanted to climb up. He bent down and scooped him onto his lap, marvelling at the solid warmth of the infant, the way he trustingly snuggled up against him before turning his attention to the bread rolls on the table.

With a laugh, Rafaello fed him while Magda sipped her coffee.

'Another day at the beach,' he announced decisively. 'That's what we all need.'

Benji would be in seventh heaven, Magda would be happy and he—well, he would have another opportunity to admire her swimsuit...

'More coffee?'

Magda shook her head. Part of her wanted to say yes, because that would mean she could go on sitting at the table. Upstairs, Benji was fast asleep, exhausted by the pleasures of the seaside, and Rafaello had persuaded her to entrust his safety to a newly-purchased baby alarm monitor that even now relayed his deep, even breathing from its receiver beside her place.

They were still out on the terrace, even at this late hour, for the weather had turned even warmer and Magda was drinking in the glory of the Italian night sky. A scrape of metal on stone accompanied Rafaello's getting to his feet. He came around the table to her and held out his hand.

'Bedtime,' he said softly.

Her breath seemed to catch in her throat. She knew exactly what he wanted—and she knew with all her heart, with all her body, that she wanted it, too. She wanted to feel his arms around her again, feel that hard, lean body against hers, feel his hands, his mouth...his tongue... moving over her, taking her step by step back to that wonderful, ecstatic, unbelievable, heavenly paradise he had taken her to last night.

'I have waited all day,' he went on, looking down at her with his dark, velvet wanting eyes. 'For countless, agonising hours…waiting for this moment, *cara*, when I would take your hand and draw you to your feet, like this—' with soft, insistent force he drew her up '—and wind my arms around you, like this—' his arms folded her against him '—and lift your face to mine and taste, ah, taste again that honey from your mouth—like this—'

His mouth lowered to hers, and with a little sigh she gave her lips to his.

It was bliss, it was heaven, it was the stars moving in a slow, insistent arc across the sable sky as his mouth moved upon hers, opening her like a flower, to feast on the nectar he sought.

'Come,' he said again, 'it is time for the night to begin…'

Could it really be, she thought, her mind a mist, her body a soft velvet fire, as good again as it had been before? And yet it was—and more. As he swept her inside his bedroom she did not even go through to check on Benji— 'He is fine, *cara*—listen, I have brought the monitor with me—he sleeps like an angel.' Rafaello breathed into her mouth as he kissed her again and again, and with each kiss, each touch, lit flames in every portion of her body, peeling from her the flimsy covering of her clothes until once again she stood naked in his embrace.

He lowered her gently to the bed, parting her legs and coming down, quite as naked as she, upon her.

'*Dio*, I will be as gentle as I can, but the waiting has been hard—'

He arched over her, his lean body like a perfect bow, eager to find its mark, his mouth plundering hers, then moving down to capture each peaking breast as his hands swept down over her slender body. Hungrily he sought the ripening core of her body, preparing it for himself—preparing her for him. At his touch she moaned, incoherent with the desire rushing through her.

His words echoed her own longing. 'I want you so much—right now...'

She was like a pale flame beneath him, burning like a lens, reflecting all her heat into him, his body.

'Rafaello—'

'Yes—say my name. I want to hear it—want to hear you cry it out aloud, to me, now, right now—'

He held her poised beneath him and then, as if of their own accord, her hips lifted to his, gyrating very slightly, feeling his hard, powerful length ready to pierce her. He needed no second invitation, and with a low growl he thrust within her.

And then her body was welcoming him, remembering him, moving around him, beneath him, clasping him to her so that he groaned again and lifted his head from her.

'*Dio*—what are you doing to me? How can I hold back? *Cara*—come with me—I must...'

He surged within her, and as if a match had been thrown into driest tinder she scorched into flame around him. A cry was wrenched from her throat, an answering cry from his, and he thrust, and thrust again as she lifted her hips to him, every muscle straining. Her head was thrown back, her eyes closing tight shut as wave after wave of sensation broke like an unstoppable tide through her.

His possession was total—as was hers of him. She clasped him to her, her hands folding and unfolding on his smooth, muscled back, her arms reaching across its broadness as she held him to her and he surged to the very utmost of her limits.

'Rafaello! Rafaello—'

It was a dying fall, a homage to him, to his beauty, to his possession, to her desire for him—and his for her, which seemed so wondrous she could not believe it was really true. And yet it was true. As the tide of sensation gave one final, blissful breaking through her convulsing body she knew, *knew* that the intensity of what she had felt had been as strong for him as it had for her. He had wanted her, desired her as she had desired him, and the wonder of it, the glory of it, made her weak.

For a long, timeless while they lay together, wound in each other's arms, no words left, no words possible. She wanted nothing more in all the world.

She must hold this moment, hold it for ever—this sweetness of bliss, this wonder of joy that was filling her and flooding her.

I love you...

The words formed on her lips, welling out of her heart, and she felt their power and their glory. But they were silent words, breathed into his living skin, into her soul.

I love you...

A silent promise. A secret gift.

'Rafaello! No. Someone might see!'

'Who? There is no one for miles.'

'Shepherds—farmers—people on holiday.'

He grinned, a wolfish parting of his teeth. 'There's not a soul around, *cara*, no one to save you from me.'

He rolled her over on the rug, spread beneath shady chestnut trees in this most remote spot, a sheltered slope with no habitation for miles. One by one he spread her hands above her head and arched his body over her.

'No one to save you from me,' he echoed, the smile on his mouth, the expression on his eyes, all portending one intention only.

She gazed helplessly back into his eyes.

'I don't want to be saved,' she breathed.

'*Bene*—the very words I want to hear,' he told her. Slowly, infinitely slowly, he kissed her, and she thought she would die of it, it was such bliss. He drew back a little, still arched over her, his palms pressed onto hers. Then he kissed her again, his warm, wine-sweetened mouth moving with leisurely exploration. She felt desire stir yet again, and wondered at it.

They had spent all morning in bed together. She had woken to discover that once again Rafaello had woken before her, and whisked Benji off to Maria. But this morning instead of bringing him back to Magda he had returned alone, informing her that Maria was taking Benji to play with her infant great-nieces, and that he would be happy and entertained and not miss her for a moment—which was highly convenient, as it happened, because right now Magda would have no time, no time at all, for paying attention to anyone else but him...

In the shuttered bedroom Rafaello had done what he had wanted to do the day before—kept Magda entirely and absolutely to himself, feasting and feeding on her without satiation, without end. It had been a sensual overload that had melted every fibre of her body, dissolving the hours in endless, timeless bliss until at last Rafaello had risen from his bed and declared it was time, finally, to get up for the day.

If that had been his intent it had been unwise, thought Magda, of him to have suggested that, since they were both in the bathroom at the same time, they might therefore shower together...

It had been a long, long shower...

And now, after a luscious picnic in the most remote spot Rafaello could find, she realised with a sigh of pleasure just what he had in mind.

To make love in the open air, beneath a bower of green leaves, the soft, warm breeze sighing in the grass, was to be Adam and Eve, she thought, in the garden of paradise. As her needless fears of discovery melted in the irresistible solvent of desire she gave herself to him in the dappled sunlight, gave herself utterly and entirely, all her being, all her heart and soul.

She loved him, she knew. Knew that it could not be otherwise, that she was helpless against its power. And whilst the bliss and glory of it filled her, far below, in the deep recesses of her being, she knew it was not for her.

Today and tomorrow she could have—whatever time was to be allotted to her to have and to hold this most beautiful of men, this most cherished of beings by her side, in her arms. She did not know why he had chosen to change towards her, had no answer for it beyond, perhaps, curiosity, whim, an impulse he had decided to indulge. But she knew, however, that it would not last—could not last—that it was some kind of dream out of time, a brief, impermanent visitation of bliss that would flame like marsh fire before extinguishing itself.

But she did not care. As she lay beneath him, her eyes staring up at the mesh of chestnut leaves above them, his sated body heavy on her, folded closely to her in her clasping arms, she knew that she did not care that it would not last—could not last—that the end would come, and that she would wake one morning to his final kiss, his last embrace.

She felt his weight lift from her as he levered himself up from her a little, shifting his weight onto one elbow. Her eyes flickered to his and she gazed at him, helpless with her love for him.

She hoped he did not see it. Hoped it did not show.

Idly he plucked a long blade of grass and trailed it along the side of her cheek. The slight tickling sensation after all she had just felt made her smile.

'Why do you smile?' he asked softly, smiling back at her as he spoke.

'Because I am happy,' she told him simply.

His smile deepened.

'So am I, *cara mia*, so am I.' He kissed her gently. 'Very happy.'

For a long, close moment they just looked at each other. Looked deep into each other's eyes. After all they had just shared—the absolute union of their bodies, the journey they had taken together to the country of passion and desire, then the flow back to this, a gentler, less tempestuous union, but still a union—Magda knew with a deep, abiding certainty that was far closer than all that had gone before. As she gazed into his eyes, and he into hers, she felt a living bond flow between them...a wondrous, living bond...

And then, as a tiny, unknown bud of emotion began to unfurl deep within her—an emotion she dared not acknowledge, dared not give a name to—she saw his eyes veil. Withdrawing from her.

The moment was gone, and so was the emotion.

It had been hope, and it had just slipped away.

They took Benji with them on their next picnic, the following day, and although Rafaello had to forgo the pleasures of love in the open air in exchange for the pleasure of seeing Magda and her son enjoying themselves, he more than made up for it on their return to the villa, as the sun was lowering over the Tyrrhenian Sea.

With almost indecent haste he handed Benji over to Maria, who had come bustling out of her domain at their arrival, slipped his hand over Magda's and simply said, 'Vene,' heading with her to the staircase.

Quite unable to meet Maria's eye, merely able to pat Benji's head and tell him to be a good boy—'He is always good, signora,' Maria assured her, with approval in her voice—Magda let herself be led upstairs.

She had the feeling that Maria's approval was not just for Benji's behaviour, but for theirs. Ever since Rafaello had transformed her from an ugly duckling the housekeeper had radiated approval upon them both. Rafaello she fussed over like a boy on his birthday, and presented him with enough food at mealtimes to fatten him for Christmas—not that it ever made the slightest difference to his greyhound leanness, Magda thought, her eyes lingering on his smooth, hard torso as he slipped his shirt from his shoulders with clear intent. And as for her, Maria simply beamed at her whenever she looked at her, saying nothing—but her eyes were eloquent.

And Magda knew why. She knew Maria thought that something *real* was happening here. That this strange, temporary marriage was becoming real.

But it wasn't. She knew that. Knew that deep, deep in her bones, in her heart, in her mind, in her soul. As he stepped towards her, the shuttered light in the bedroom making his body bronze, she knew that Rafaello was merely intrigued by her, that he was still caught up in the unexpected pleasure of having turned her into, if not a swan, then at least a graceful songbird—a little street sparrow he had touched with gold and taught to fly.

And she was flying now. Lifting on wings of passion as he stroked her sun-warmed skin and murmured soft Italian words to her, bent to taste the sweetness of her mouth and carry her to his bed as together they began to soar towards the all-consuming sun and burn within its fiery heart.

Afterwards he held her close, his arm around her, and she rested her head upon his chest. His fingers played idly with her hair. They said nothing, but in the silence Magda found a peace she had never known before.

He took her out for dinner that evening, after Benji was asleep and Maria had been entrusted with the baby monitor—not that she didn't cast it a jaundiced look, Magda noted with a smile—and they dined in a formidably elegant restaurant with a wonderful view over the valley beyond. Magda sat there feeling like a princess in her blue silk gown with diamonds around her neck.

But it was Rafaello who made her feel like a princess, not the designer gown or the priceless diamonds—Rafaello. The man she loved. But because she knew that princesses only lived in fairytales, not real life, she knew that although she was not the ugly duckling any more, she was still Cinderella—and the hands of the clock were edging towards midnight.

She did not know when it would strike. Did not know how long Rafaello would continue to be intrigued by her, diverted by his own unexpected magic trick of turning a drab, downtrodden char into a woman worthy of his attention—worthy of his bed. She knew he would never be harsh to her, never discard her cruelly, but she knew, with a deep, terrible certainty, that one day the phone would ring, or an e-mail would arrive, or his father would return, or he would simply remember that his real life had nothing to do with the woman he had hired to marry him so that he could get control of the company his father had threatened to sell under his nose.

And when it happened she would pack her bags, and pick up Benji, and take one last, long look at the man who held her heart in his hands—a gift he had never asked for, would never even know he possessed—and go back to *her* real life, taking with her nothing but memories, every one of them a priceless, precious jewel to treasure all her days.

'What is it?'

His voice was low, penetrating her thoughts.

She made herself smile, lifting her wine glass. 'Nothing. I was pitying people back in Britain. I saw an English newspaper headline that said it was the wettest June for years.'

Rafaello gave an answering smile. 'Don't think about wet English summers—only glorious Tuscan ones!'

She set down her glass. 'I'll remember this summer all my life—thank you, Rafaello. Thank you from the bottom of my heart.' She met his eyes, pouring into her expression all her gratitude to him for granting her this magical fairytale to live in for a little while.

Something flickered in his eyes. She could not tell what

it was. He gave a little bow of his head, an oddly formal gesture.

'It was my pleasure, *cara*. And still is...' He reached across the table and took her hand in his, lifted it to his mouth. His kiss was soft—his eyes softer.

Magda felt her heart still, and just for a moment completely cease to beat. Then, as she gazed wordlessly at him, it happened again. His expression was veiled and he set her hand free.

'Tomorrow,' he announced, 'I show you Firenze.'

A weight pressed against Magda's heart as she continued with her meal.

Florence was magnificent. The Italian Renaissance made visible in stone and marble, oil and fresco, so rich with treasures of art and architecture that it left Magda reeling.

And yet it oppressed her. Or something did. As she gazed at the glories of the Uffizi she found herself longing again for that magical day in Lucca, when Rafaello had waved his magic wand over her and she had appeared to him for the first, most wondrous time in all her life, pleasing as a woman...

She did her best to hide her inner oppression. Not just because she knew she had no right to make him feel uncomfortable about her in any way—he had never asked her to fall in love with him, never wanted her to—but because it would simply waste one of these most precious golden days with him.

So she smiled, and feasted her eyes upon him, and revelled at the closeness of his body to hers, the casual wrap of his arm around her shoulder, the way he held her hand as they gazed at the glories of the Renaissance masters. And she crushed down the dull foreboding deep within her.

They were taking time out with a much needed coffee on one of the *piazzas*—Magda half watching the world go by, half watching the way the sinews of Rafaello's bare forearm with its rolled back shirtsleeve combined such a miraculous artistry of strength and grace as his hand covered hers warmly—when someone approached them.

'Rafaello! *Ciao!*' A stream of Italian followed, and Magda saw that the chicly dressed female greeting Rafaello was Lucia. Hovering at her side was a louche young man with tight curls and full lips.

Rafaello returned the greeting civilly, and Lucia turned her attention to Magda.

'So, you have been enjoying Tuscany to the full?' Her voice was pleasant enough, and Magda nodded, making an appropriate reply.

Lucia's head tilted very slightly in Rafaello's direction.

'And all that Tuscany has to offer you, I expect—no?'

This time there was a clear alternative meaning to her words. Magda found herself slipping her hand away from under Rafaello's and managed merely to smile slightly, as if she did not understand what Lucia had been so obviously referring to. The woman shrugged slightly.

'Well, enjoy what you can while you can. Now, do please excuse me—Carlo is impatient to show me his latest masterpiece.'

She tucked her arm proprietorially into the young man's, and with an elegant little wave took her leave.

Something that sounded like a dismissive rasp sounded in Rafaello's throat.

'*Dio*, to think she ever thought I would marry her!' He glanced contemptuously at the man at his cousin's side.

'She doesn't seem to be pining for you,' Magda agreed. Lucia was leaning into her lover now, making it clear that was exactly what he was.

Rafaello's eyes suddenly flicked to hers.

'And you, *cara*, would you pine for me?'

The question had come out of the blue. Magda froze. She dipped her head, unable to meet Rafaello's eyes.

'I...I don't think you'd want me to pine for you, would you?'

Her reply was low-voiced, but she tried hard to make it unemotional. As she finished speaking she made herself lift her eyes again, keeping her expression steady.

He was silent a moment, and for that instant he looked into her eyes and she could not read his expression. She felt frozen still.

Then, with a little shake of his head, he said, 'No, I wouldn't want you to pine for me.'

There was a note in his voice she did not know. It seemed to her to be a warning. She slipped her gaze past his, towards the medieval church on the far side of the busy *piazza*.

How much human happiness and sorrow its stones must have seen—and mine is just one more...

The thought should have brought her comfort.

But it did not.

She knew at once the next morning that something was wrong. When she woke Rafaello was standing by the window, looking out over the beautiful gardens of the villa, bathed in early sunlight. He had his back to her and he was wearing the same business suit he had worn the day he'd married her. It made him look dark, and forbidding.

As he heard her stir, he turned. His figure was outlined against the brightness of the day outside, and it came to her that it was earlier than they usually woke.

'Magda?' His voice was querying. Then, realising she was awake, he crossed to the bed. He looked taller, more austere as he looked down at her, freshly shaven and with his hair subdued into crisp businesslike neatness.

'I must go to Rome. The board meeting takes place today and I must be there.'

His voice was clipped, his tone impersonal. The Rafaello she had come to know and love so deeply seemed a million miles away. In his place was the man who had paid her to marry him, hired her for a job he could find no one else to do. Something chilled inside her. Oh, she knew he was not always this man—knew that the Rafaello who had made her a fairytale princess was there still—but not today. Not this morning. This Rafaello had put the other one aside—it was time to go back to his real life.

'Oh,' she heard herself say blankly, lifting herself clumsily onto her elbow, keeping the bedclothes around her. 'Of course.'

He went on looking down at her. There was something formidable about him standing there, looking like the rich powerful businessman he was, as remote and alien as when she had first laid eyes on him, cleaning his bathroom on her knees.

A frown creased between his eyes. He started to rotate the gold cufflink on his left wrist.

'When I come back,' he said abruptly, 'we must talk. You understand that, *cara*?'

She nodded. A lump had formed in her throat, hard and choking like an unswallowable stone.

'Yes—'

His mouth tightened. 'We have been living in a dream, these days together...'

The stone swelled in her throat. 'Yes—'

She tried to hide her expression, desperate for him not to see what she was terrified must be there. He stood looking down at her, his expression troubled. Then, with a sudden softening of his eyes, he spoke, and for a moment it was Rafaello back again, the man who took her to paradise and held her in his arms.

'I will take care of you, *cara*—be assured.'

Then, twisting his wrist, he glanced at his watch and gave a rasp of displeasure.

'I have to go—'

He bent swiftly, leaning his arm against the wall, and dropped on her mouth one last, hurried kiss.

And was gone.

CHAPTER TEN

MAGDA was at the pool with Benji. Her heart was heavy. Rafaello couldn't have made it clearer that this golden, magical time was over. Again and again she heard his words echoing in her head—*When I come back we must talk.*

They tolled like a funeral bell against all her happiness. She did not need to be clairvoyant to know what it was he wanted to talk to her about. Rafaello's real life had reclaimed him—the real life that consisted of him being a driven, powerful businessman, with important things to do in the world far beyond dallying with a woman he had never intended to dally with in the first place.

She had known it would happen eventually. Yet all the knowledge in the world about just how temporary her bliss could be did not make its impending loss any easier to bear. Her sense of oppression thickened, bowing her like a physical weight.

The sharp click of heels upon the stone path approaching the pool area made her turn her head. Her gaze froze as she saw Lucia approaching her. What was she doing here? Every instinct told Magda her arrival was not happy.

'Magda—I have bad news.' The other woman's voice was staccato, and for a second Magda bristled. Then, a second later, she realised Lucia was not being hostile—her face was stiff with shock.

'Enrico has had a heart attack!'

A gasp escaped Magda, and she stood up from the shaded lounger, sliding Benji to his feet.

The other woman ploughed on. 'He has been taken to

hospital. Rafaello is with him. They do not know if he can live—'

She broke off with a choke.

Magda stood there, not knowing what to say. Oh, poor, poor Rafaello, she thought—what agony for him.

'I'm so sorry,' she heard herself say in a whisper. She took a breath, feeling helpless as she said it, but knowing she must, 'Is there anything…anything I can do?'

Lucia looked at her. She nodded.

'This is difficult for me to say.' She paused, then went on, 'I do not say this in enmity, you must understand that— but…' She paused again, then continued, 'The best thing you can do now is go.'

For a moment Magda thought she meant go to Rome, to Rafaello, and then, as if a knife were suddenly slicing into her heart, she realised that was not what his cousin meant.

The expression on Lucia's face was troubled, and she seemed to find what she was saying uncomfortable.

'Enrico needs Rafaello—and Rafaello needs Enrico. I once thought…' She hesitated, then continued, 'I once thought that the way to bring them together again was through Rafaello marrying me. I was mistaken. Rafaello merely saw it as his father's ploy to control him—and he will not be controlled. You, of all people, know the ends he went to in order to escape being controlled by his father. But now—Enrico may die. He must make his peace with his son—and Rafaello with his father.' She looked Magda straight in the eyes. 'They cannot make their peace if you are still here. You must see that.'

The knife was still slicing through Magda's heart. But through the pain she heard the inescapable logic of what Lucia was telling her.

'I must be able to tell Enrico—if he still lives—that you are gone. Then he can make his peace with his son.'

The pain was so bad Magda did not know how she was

bearing it. As if it were visible in her face, Lucia spoke again. Her voice was kinder this time.

'I know it will be hard for you. You have fallen in love with my cousin. No, do not deny it—it was obvious from the start that you would do so. How could you not? To you Rafaello is like some prince out of a fairytale. But, though you will not thank me for saying so, he should not have awakened you with his kisses. While you were...as you were when you first came here...you were safe from him. But now...' She sighed. 'Oh, Rafaello does not understand—he never has. Girls have been falling in love with him all his life. He does not mean to be cruel, but he just does not see it happening.' She gave a little shrug. 'That was why I thought a marriage between us might work—I know him too well to fall in love with him, so he could never have hurt me.'

She looked at Magda. Her dark eyes were not unsympathetic. 'You did not believe it meant anything to him, did you? You did not think that it could last, this brief affair?'

The pain was running down every limb of Magda's body. She tried to fight it, desperate to deny what Lucia was saying to her despite the resonance it found so readily in her own heart.

'I can't just go—without Rafaello's say-so. He may not want me to go yet...'

Even as she spoke she knew she was deceiving herself. Rafaello was not concerned with her now—he was concerned only, as he should be, with his father.

Lucia was taking something out of her handbag, something pale that fluttered as she held it out to Magda.

'He asked me to give you this.' Her voice was strained and she would not quite meet Magda's eyes. As she took the piece of paper and looked at it Magda knew why.

It was a cheque. It was made out to her—for ten thousand euros. As she stared, her heart crushed in a vice that squeezed the blood from every pore, Rafaello's strong, black signature wavered in front of her eyes.

Lucia was speaking again.

Magda forced herself to listen, though inside herself she could hear only a terrifying, deafening silence that just went on and on without end.

'Rafaello said…' The woman hesitated again, as if only too aware what Magda must be going through. 'Said that he would be in touch later, to sort everything out. But that right now his first duty is to his father. He hopes you will understand…' Her voice trailed off. 'I'm sorry, my dear. You see, he won't have realised what you have come to feel for him. For him this marriage was always just a…business transaction.'

Magda could say nothing—nothing except a dull, broken assent. The crushing weight in her heart was agony.

Lucia was saying something again, glancing at her watch.

'Forgive me, I do not mean to…upset you further, but I have merely stopped here on my way to the airport. I am catching the next flight to Rome, so that I can be with Tio Enrico if…if he still lives.' There was a strain in her voice Magda could not ignore. 'If it will not take you long to pack, I can take you to the airport with me. Rafaello has asked me to arrange your ticket and so forth.'

She looked pityingly at Magda, still standing there, Benji at her side gazing uncomprehendingly, clinging to his mother's leg.

'It would be best not to linger.' Her voice was as pitying as her expression.

With feet of lead, Magda collected her things and headed indoors.

It was raining. Rain pattered on the thin roof of the caravan, splattered on the glass in the windows. Benji whined irritably at Magda's knee.

'I know, muffin, it's horrid—all this rain. Perhaps to-morrow will be sunny.'

A gust of wind caught the caravan. It was old, shabby inside, and no one wanted to rent it on the beachside site. But that was what made it cheap—cheap enough to hire for a month in high season. Cheap enough to buy.

The enormity of what she was planning to do swept over Magda again, but she put her doubts aside. The south coast seaside just had to be a better place to raise Benji. There was nothing for her in London—her bedsit was gone, and so was her job.

There's nothing for me anywhere…

Angrily she pushed the despairing thought aside. That wasn't true; she still had Benji.

She stroked his head and opened up the jigsaw box, tipping out the pieces. Refusing to let the memories come back.

They came all the same, crowding in, impossible to push away.

Rafaello. So impossibly beautiful, so impossible not to adore. Rafaello holding her in his arms, smiling at her, laughing with her, kissing her. Making love to her.

It wasn't love. It was just an affair for him—a dalliance. She had known from the start it must end.

More memories rushed in, though she tried even harder to keep them out. But they pushed in, piercing her like knives.

One final memory, from the last time she had set eyes on him. He'd stood there, looking down at her, his face grave. *I shall take care of you—*

Well, he had. He had taken care of her. Made sure she had gone home with what she came for. Money.

That was why she'd married him. For money. Money to make a home for Benji. Not for love, for money.

She hadn't wanted to cash his cheque, had resisted for two weeks while she lived on the money she had got back from the airline company at Pisa airport after exchanging Lucia's business class ticket for a humbler fare. She'd landed at Gatwick, not Heathrow, and on impulse had taken the train to the south coast, found a caravan camp which still had vacancies this wet summer.

But now she needed Rafaello's pay-off to buy the caravan outright—make a home for herself and Benji, however humble—and have a nest egg to tide her over for a while. As for the rest of the money Rafaello had promised her—she knew she could never take it.

Just as she had not been able to take the clothes he had bought for her, nor the gold necklace he had given her. Besides, they would hardly fit her lifestyle now.

She smiled, painful though it was to do so. At least she had her memories.

They would need to last a lifetime.

Across the shingle the grey tide churned the pebbles, plucking and knocking. Benji was crouched down, picking up the shiny sea-wet stones. His feet were in wellingtons, his little figure clad in a waterproof jacket. Rain swept in from the west, slanting in chill, unrelenting strokes that stung her cheeks and blurred her vision.

Magda stared across the bleak, drear English Channel. Far out to sea was an oil tanker, ploughing its slow way eastwards. There were no sailboats today, hardly anyone on the beach. She had ventured out because she could stay indoors no longer. Benji was pettish, refusing to be entertained by anything. She was restless, heart aching like an ague in her bones.

Day by day the reality of it was sinking in. Rafaello had gone from her life. Gone completely. Gone as abruptly as he had come.

Sternly she tried to pull herself together. She had no right to mope like this. She was blessed with Benji, she had her health, her strength—a home of her own. This would be a good place to bring up Benji—fresh air, and the seaside on her doorstep....

And here, at least, she could stand in the rain and the wind blowing up the Channel and stare southwards, towards Italy, with a hopeless longing in her heart never to be fulfilled.

Her cheeks were wet. But not with rain.

Benji picked up one last stone, and threw it with all his tiny might into the sea. It landed with a plop that was quite inaudible in the noisy surf. Then, bored, he turned and tottered off.

Magda followed him, hugging her anorak around her, facing into the endless rain. Her booted feet crunched the shingle, slowing her down. Raindrops spat in her face. As she pushed back her wind-whipped hair, twisting her neck to try and refasten it into the clip it had escaped from, she stilled. And stared.

On the shingle shelf, above the high tide, a figure stood. Quite immobile.

She blinked. Something caught at her.

She reached for Benji's hand blindly, halting him. She went on staring landwards. The figure at the top of the beach started to walk towards her. A gust of wind buffeted her and she hung on to Benji's hand to steady him. And went on staring.

Time was slowing down. Slowing right, right down. The rain seemed to be stopping, slowing and stilling in mid flight. The wind dropped.

Silence drummed all around her. She felt Benji's fingers pressing into hers. Felt him tugging her. She was unresponsive. Her feet were leaden; she could not move.

Nor could she breathe. The air was solid in her lungs.

The figure kept on walking towards her.

His face resolved itself, through the rain, through the blurring of her vision.

She couldn't move. Couldn't breathe.

Then, suddenly, Benji's hand pulled free of hers. She saw him totter forwards, arms outstretched.

'Ra—' he said. 'Ra—pick up!'

Rafaello picked him up.

'Hello, Benji,' he said.

Then he looked at Magda. His dark eyes pierced her like a knife, cutting straight into her heart.

'Come home,' he said. He held out his free hand to her. 'Come home, *cara*.'

She didn't move, couldn't move.

'I don't understand.' Her words were a whisper, lost in the wind.

His mouth twisted. 'Nor did I. Not when I came back from Rome that night, to find you gone. Not when Maria took one look at me and threw up her hands, saying that you had set off after me that very morning. It made no sense. And then she said you'd had a lift—a lift from a very helpful visitor.' His face darkened. 'And when she told me who your visitor had been—then I understood.' His eyes shut, lashes sweeping long, before opening again. '*Dio!* When I heard that I understood, all right!'

She was swaying in the wind. It went right through her bones, scouring her heart.

'How—how is your father?'

'My father? Ah, yes, my father.' His voice was heavy. 'Making an excellent recovery, you will be glad to know— from his non-existent heart attack.'

She stared.

His mouth twisted again. 'My father has the constitution of an ox. Don't you see? Lucia lied to you.'

'Why?' Her voice was faint.

'*Why?* To get rid of you, of course!'

She swallowed. Her voice was painful. 'She could have waited another day, then. It would have saved her a journey.'

A frown darkened his brow. Carefully he set Benji down

again, and while the little boy fell with glee upon a gleaming shell he straightened and demanded, '*Non capisco?* What do you mean?'

Her voice didn't work properly, but she made the words come.

'You'd already warned me—that morning—that…that you were going to send me back.'

He stared. 'What is this you are saying?'

He seemed angry. She wondered why. 'You said…you said we would have to talk. I…I knew what you meant.'

There was nothing in his face. Nothing at all. Then, very carefully, he spoke.

'And what, *cara*, did I mean? Tell me.'

Her hands clenched in her pockets.

'Rafaello, please. I knew—I knew, I promise you. I knew that you were only being kind to me—that you had waved a magic wand over me and…and decided to be kind, let me have my little dream. I knew that was all it was—that it was not supposed to be more than that. I understood. I did—truly.' She swallowed, then went on. 'You gave me fair warning—that day in Florence. You warned me then that you would not want me to pine for you. I understood then.'

He looked at her. There was something strange about his face. She could not read it—but then all she wanted to do was gaze and drink him in. For this was heaven, a tiny, minuscule sliver of heaven, beamed down to her by special delivery to make another, final memory for her to keep and treasure all her days. One last joy.

She was drinking him in as a thirsty man would drink water in the desert. Drinking in his dark, beautiful eyes, his silken rain-wet hair, the beads of water on his lashes, the strong column of his nose, the planes of his face, the sculpted beauty of his mouth.

'You understood?' His voice was flat. Benji patted his knee, proffering the shell. Absently he took it, murmuring something to the child. She watched him turn the shell over in his fingers. His eyes went back to hers.

'You understood?' he said again. Then, with a savage movement he hurled the shell far out into the sea. Benji stared, open-mouthed with admiration at such might, and tried to follow suit with a pebble.

His audience were not watching.

They were kissing.

Heaven. Heaven had swept over her again, drowning her. As the shell had left his fist Rafaello had reached for her and crushed her to him.

'Then understand *this*!' he rasped, and closed his mouth over hers.

Magda's eyes fluttered shut. She was not standing on a sodden English beach, lashed with rain. She was standing beneath the Tuscan stars, with the scent of flowers all around her, the sweet Italian air in her lungs, the warm Italian night embracing her—and Rafaello—Rafaello kissing her.

She clung to him. Clung to him in desperation, in delirium, because it must be a figment of her imagination. It must be. There was no reason for him to kiss her. No reason for him to crush her so close against his lean, hard body that she felt herself fuse to him. No reason for his hands to cup her rain-wet head as if it were precious alabaster. No reason for him to speak into her mouth words she could not believe—must not believe.

He let her go.

'*Now* do you understand?' His eyes blazed down at her.

'No,' she said faintly.

'*Per Dio!* Then come—come home with me, and I will spend all my life trying to make you understand. I love you so much.'

She heard, but could not believe. He saw it in her face.

'Your doubt shames me,' he said in a low voice. 'I thought I had made it so clear to you—every night we were together. But then…' His voice dropped even lower and he took her hands in his. 'Even I did not realise what name to give my feelings for you. They were so new to me—I could not recognise them. They confused me, made me question everything. But they grew in me and grew in me until I saw them for what they were—and realised I must turn a dream into reality. That is why I said I wouldn't want you to pine for me—because there would never be a reason for you to do so. I would turn the dream into reality for us both. *That* is why I was so solemn that last morning—I knew we must make our marriage a real one and that I would have to tell my father so. Tell him that even if he never spoke to me again—severed all ties, sold the company to the first passing stranger—you would stay my wife for ever—because I had fallen in love with you and could not live another day without you.'

She felt faint again, but it was bliss running through her, taking the breath from her body.

'Did you truly not see it?' he asked, looking down at her with disbelief in his eyes.

'How could I? How could I think such a miracle would happen to me?' There was wonder in her voice.

He smiled, and his smile was an embrace. 'You are my miracle, Magda. You and Benji. You crept into my heart, the pair of you, day by day, and now you are there for ever. My love for you was in my eyes, my touch.' His expression changed. 'Lucia saw it that day in Firenze—saw that we were in love with each other. And she knew she had found a way of revenging herself for my rejection of her. She determined to part us. So she came to you with that story of Enrico's collapse—oh, yes, I got the truth out of her, spitting and snarling though she was by the time I managed it. Lies, every word of it.'

'But…but the cheque? She gave me a cheque from you…'

A growl rasped from his throat. 'A forgery! She had gone

through my desk to find a chequebook before seeking you out. She knew it would convince you that I indeed wanted you to leave Italy right away.' His face shadowed. 'How could you believe her lies, *cara*?'

'She played on my fears,' said Magda achingly.

His mouth thinned. 'Just as she played on my father's obsession for a grandchild and my own obsession with the company. Trying to manipulate us all. Well—' his voice hardened '—that is over now. I have warned her that if she ever tries to make trouble again I will press charges for fraud. But,' he went on, his voice softening, 'that cheque did give me the means of finding you at last.'

Magda stared, not understanding. He gave her a wry smile. 'I stopped the cheque as a forgery, *cara*. My bank informed me the moment it was presented for payment, and at which bank. That's how I traced you.' His voice changed again. 'You do not know what I have been through—every day has been an eternity without you.'

He pressed her hands so tightly that the pressure should have hurt. But she could feel no pain. Only a happiness so deep, so absolute that it consumed her very being. How could fairytales come true?

She looked at him, and all the love she had for him blazed from her eyes.

He kissed her again, in sweet possession, and she folded against him. As his arms wrapped around her, holding her so close she could feel his heart beating next to hers, one last doubt assailed her.

'Rafaello?' She lifted her face, eyes troubled.

He smoothed her hair. *'Si?'*

'Your father—?'

'—is perfectly well. I told you—Lucia lied to you.'

'No—I meant—I…I don't want to come between you.'

He brushed her brow with his lips.

'You have brought us together—finally, after so many stupid, stubborn years.'

She looked at him questioningly.

'When he saw my despair when I could not find you, my grief at losing you, something broke between us—that cruel, hard wall that had separated us for so long. You see…' There was a catch in his voice as he went on, 'I was reminding him of himself—fifteen years ago—when my mother died.'

She felt her hand clutch at him more tightly.

'I didn't know—'

'Her death drove us apart. It shouldn't have—but it did. I went…wild. I can see that now. And my father…he simply locked himself away inside himself. We both of us grieved—but we could not reach out to each other, father to son, to comfort each other. And once the wall was built between us, neither of us could undo it. Until now. It's thanks to you, my beloved heart, that I have my father back as well.'

But still she was troubled. 'He can't want me—'

'*Si!*' He took a breath. 'I told him, Magda—I told him everything about you. How you took a dying woman's child to care for and love, how your loyalty to your friend, your love for a motherless child, made you put aside your own life, whatever it cost you. And he was as stricken with remorse as I was—he begs your forgiveness, *cara*. And he asks you if you will accept this, and wear it every day— for him and for me.'

He reached inside his pocket and drew out an antique ring box. There, inside, was a ring glistening with diamonds and sapphires.

'It is the eternity ring my mother wore—my father gave it to her as a symbol of his undying love. And I give it to you—' there was another catch in his voice and Magda's throat tightened in response '—as a symbol of my undying love for you.'

He slipped it on her finger and the tears spilled out of her eyes.

'Let us be happy for ever,' he said softly, and kissed her quietly, lovingly, with all his heart.

There was a tug at his leg.

'Pick up!' demanded a little voice.

Rafaello stooped and scooped up the little boy and hugged him close. And the three of them stood there, in the pouring rain, in the gusting wind, beside the cold grey sea, their arms around each other.

My family, thought Magda, and her heart turned over.

Rafaello hefted Benji onto his shoulders. The little boy squealed with glee and clutched his bearer's hair.

'Ouch!' said Rafaello. 'Benji—don't pull Papà's hair. Now you are my son you must be nice to me.'

He started to walk towards the shore.

'Come on,' he called to Magda. 'We have a flight to catch. My father is desperate to make amends to you, Maria and my aunt are desperate to get Benji to themselves again, and I—I am just desperate for you!'

With the crunch of shingle under her feet she hurried after them, her husband and her son. Her heart was singing, and it was a song that would never end.

The world's bestselling romance series.

HARLEQUIN®
Presents~
Seduction and Passion Guaranteed!

FROM BOARDROOM
TO BEDROOM

**Harlequin Presents® brings you two
original stories guaranteed to make
your Valentine's Day extra special!**

THE BOSS'S
MARRIAGE ARRANGEMENT
by *Penny Jordan*

Pretending to be her boss's mistress is one thing—but now
everyone in the office thinks Harriet is Matthew Cole's
fiancée! Harriet has to keep reminding herself it's all just
for convenience, but how far is Matthew prepared to go
with the arrangement—marriage?

HIS DARLING VALENTINE
by *Carole Mortimer*

It's Valentine's Day, but Tazzy Darling doesn't care.
Until a secret admirer starts bombarding her with gifts!
Any woman would be delighted—but not Tazzy. There's
only one man she wants to be sending her love tokens, and
that's her boss, Ross Valentine. And her secret admirer
couldn't possibly be Ross…could it?

The way to a man's heart…is through the bedroom

www.eHarlequin.com

HPFBTB0205

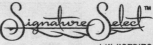

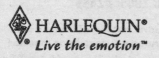

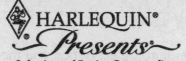